Pangyrus

Pangyrus © 2020
All Stories © 2020
Attributed to the authors named herein, except when noted otherwise
under "Acknowledgements"
ISBN: 978-0-9979164-5-4

All rights reserved
Printed in the United States of America
First published in 2020

For information about permission to reproduce selections from this book,
please write to Permissions at info@pangyrus.com

The text of this book is set in Palatino
with display text set in Crimson and Baskerville
Composition by Abraar Chaudhry
Cover design by Doug Woodhouse

Editor: Greg Harris
Managing Editor: Cynthia Bargar
Print Edition Manager: Susan Wyssen
Fiction Editors: Anne Bernays, Erica Boyce Murphy
Poetry Editor: Cheryl Clark Vermeulen
Nonfiction Editor: E.B. Bartels
Food Writing Editor: Deborah Norkin
Science Editor: Mona Tousian
Comics Editor: Dan Mazur
Reviews Editor: Chris Hartman
Special Projects Editor: Virginia Pye
Graphic & Web Designer: Esther Weeks
Social Media: Yahya Chaudhry
Readers and Copy Editors: Dee Costello, Chris Hartman, Molly Howes,
Jess McCann, Rachel Darke, Brittany Capozzi, Bahz Iannoli, Judy Kessler,
Indu Shanmugam, Akiko Yamagata, Artress Bethany White
Editorial Assistants: Suzannah Lutz, Jessica Goodwin
Logo Design: Ted Ollier
Pangyrus
79 JFK Street, L103
Cambridge, MA 02138
pangyrus.com

Contents

Note from the Editor   9

Nonfiction/Essay
Find Everything You Are Looking For? by Grace Segran   47
Appetite by Kat Read   Z*EST!*   56
Off. by Lauren Marie Scovel   77
Paul Laurence Dunbar Reveals How We All Wear the Mask
    by Chris Hartman   84
Pastries in the Backcountry by Tanushree Baidya   113
Chance that Mimics Choice by V. N. Alexander   S*CIENCE*   128
The Secret Life of an Old Maine Shoe
    by Christina Marsden Gillis   154
Reciprocal Identities by Andrea Caswell   S*CIENCE*   174
Butter by Joy Cooke   Z*EST!*   183
Chisinau, 2017 by Flora Lindsay-Herrera   199

Poetry
Chronically by Diannely Antigua   19
Get Off My Lawn by Tanya Larkin   20
My Nature by Tanya Larkin   23
Counting Backwards by Kevin McLellan   69
The Rise of Negation by Kevin McLellan   70
From the Inside Out by Kevin McLellan   71
Adiabatic Theorem by Suzanne S. Rancourt   82
I Likened Her Hair to a River by Myron Michael   109
Dear Life by Marisa P. Clark   111
The Most Poetic Thing by Jose Hernandez Diaz   129
Black Hole Beheld by Michael J. Leach   127
Andromeda by Martha McCollough   133
Erinys by Martha McCollough   136
Up Close by Jennifer Markell   151
It's Hard to Get a Bead on God by Jennifer Markell   152
Ends Meet by Alex Wells Shapiro   153

Johnnie Redding by Justin Danzy — 170
Legacy by Mary-Kim Arnold — 171
Northern Goshawk by Michael Hardin — 181
Eastern Owl Screech by Michael Hardin — 182
Prologue to a Stutter by Kerri Sonnenberg — 186
Forward, Thinking by Kerri Sonnenberg — 187
Appliances by Meg Yardley — 195
The Plain by Ruth Lepson — 196
Ni Pena Ni Miedo by David Green — 206

Fiction and Comics
The Novel I Will Never Write: A Screed By Gabe Cohen
    by E. Thomas Finan — 13
Lamplight on the River by Shanti Thirumalai — 26
Does the Name Blackie Donovan Mean Anything To You?
    by Ron MacLean — 61
Hash Pipe by Amy Bernstein — 73
Moose by Deborah Mead — 97
Circus Lights by Franklin Einspruch   COMIC — 138
Longing by Christie Marra — 144
The Joy of Agony by Mark Halpern — 157
Nathaniel by Jim Mentink — 189
Baking for the Masses by Zachary Spence   ZEST! — 209

Contributors — 216
About Pangyrus — 223

Pangyrus

Note from the Editor

Some plans are so well-laid they don't seem plans at all; they are habits. Going to the office to work. Having coffee with a friend. Tossing a package of toilet paper into the grocery cart.

The COVID-19 pandemic has shown us these, too, can go astray. How much more thoroughly, then, might the effort to produce a print issue unravel? For our editors, this is a labor of love, easily lost. Someone's mother dies. A partner gets nicked in the heart by a stray surgeon's scalpel. A poem resists all efforts at formatting. An editor-in-chief gets consumed by his teaching schedule.

The good news is that you, our readers, noticed when something was missing. The even better news is that finally, here before you, is Pangyrus 7.

Over the course of its production, things have—to put it mildly—changed. There's a chance you're reading it in ebook format, as our usual mailroom has been firmly shut down. A chance that you're reading it in a home that has become, instead of refuge from work, the production site of your daily job. A chance you're reading it with eyes fatigued from too many video calls.

PANGYRUS

In the early days of assembling this issue, months prior to the pandemic, print edition editor Susan Wyssen suggested an emerging theme—that many of the pieces connected to the body. It was hard to imagine then how thoroughly the world would remind us of our embodiedness, how the precondition of words is breath, and breath the very thing that the virus threatens to steal. From subtheme, that focus grew into a brand-new section, "In Sickness and In Health," launched online with a call for submissions that resulted in hundreds of new pieces. In this issue you'll find stories, poems, and essays that showed us the way—some of which read very differently now.

These include Grace Segran's "Find Everything You Are Looking For?" a reflection by a writer on the rewards of working in a drug store that turned unexpectedly timely. Tanya Larkin's "Get Off My Lawn," where the whimsy and intensity of child's play turn indoor and outdoor space into contested zones that the parents among us will recognize all too well. Kevin McLellan's "The Rise of Negation," with its stark opening observation:

> your memories like cells / these
> imperfect combinations continue
> dividing and multiplying in the
> swelter today

But a volume of Pangyrus would be a sodden thing if it made only the expected connections. We look for discovery, and our range is broad. We're thrilled to publish Ron MacLean's masterful short story, "Does the Name Blackie Donovan Mean Anything to You?," a gangster tale with a twist, and E. Thomas Finan's "The Novel I Will Never Write," a screed that every writer will ruefully recognize. Chris Hartman's review of a new documentary, "Paul Dunbar Reveals How We All Wear the Mask," bears absolutely no relationship to the pandemic masks we all wear—and yet reminds us of a history, and a struggle with identity, we might too easily lose if we focus too thinly on the present struggle.

But enough with the preview. These pages—these pixels—burst with talent; the moments captured are luminous. Read on, and discover for yourself.

—Greg Harris

The Novel I Will Never Write: A Screed By Gabe Cohen

by E. Thomas Finan

The protagonist of the novel I will never write is kind of like me. Except more articulate. And cleverer. And a bit more handsome. And, if I'm real honest, his life-story's a lot more interesting than mine. But he is about as tall as I am (6'1"), and he's about my age (25 or so).

If I scavenged my life for all my best insights, *bon mots*, and exhilarations, that would be like his average day, or at least his average week. All the comebacks that pop into my head only hours later and that stew in my skull over the next few days (the fuel for the lantern of regrets always at my shoulder)—well, they spring from his mouth at exactly the right moment. And he says them with just enough cockiness, that golden mean between pussy and dudebro.

The protagonist is a writer—like me—but he doesn't seem like some loser who writes only to get a growing list of rejections. That is, he's more Lord Byron than Gabe Cohen. He's not a novelist; his life is way too interesting to spend hours in front of the computer working on a piece of fiction. But you know that, if he did write a novel, it would be the best thing ever—like *Moby-Dick* or *The*

Recognitions or *2666*. I sometimes think that I only think of him as a writer because I want him to be the hero in every way that I'm not the hero. So he has to be a writer or at least a guy who could be a writer. He's a journalist for a place that's a cross between *VICE* and *Harper's*, and his writing is just the overflowing of his personality, with all its sparkling charisma.

Anyway, he inherits a spoon from an old Dutch silverware set that used to belong to his great-aunt or grandmother or something. The spoon leads him (long story) to this underground breakdancing ring with neo-Nazi elements that has dance-offs in parking garages around the Northeast. Our hero resolves to get to the bottom of this world of breakdancing fascists and find the rest of the silverware set, so he becomes one of the top dancers (handle: *Spenser Z*). The novel culminates in a trip to Chile—a sort of world finals—where our hero finds the rest of the silverware set, discovers an old war criminal, and, of course, gets the girl. Well, he doesn't really *get* her because *getting the girl* is probably a bit misogynistic, and I don't want to write one of those trite love stories where lovers walk hand in hand into the horizon. But she's a computer-programming whiz who helps him crack the secrets of this breakdancing ring with neo-Nazi elements (again, it's a long story). She also may or may not be a relative of Simon Wiesenthal. So he and she end the novel on a Santiago rooftop, and, as they stare at the mountains, you, perceptive reader, will get the sense that maybe they could have a future together.

Of course, I don't know how I, as a writer, will get you, as reader, to *get the sense that maybe they could have a future together*.

I could do it through dialogue: *So, you want to have dinner or something?*

Or maybe through the description of the scenery: *The Andes seemed like the threshold of a new horizon for both of them.*

Or maybe through narration: *She stowed her submachine gun in his bag as the Cessna flew north.*

I don't know because, of course, I haven't gotten to the end yet. If I had gotten to the end, it would no longer be *the novel I will never write* but instead *the mediocre novel I just finished*. And the latter really is a terrifying idea!

This is my third never-written novel. I've typed hundreds of pages that will never be a novel. And sometimes I can't tell which pages belong in which novel. It's like I've been working on the limbs of the same novel for the past five years. And, no matter how much I stitch and cut, those bloody stumps just continue to lie there.

Here's the thing about the novel I will never write: all the good parts are derivative, and all the original parts are mediocre. Look at even the précis a few paragraphs back. American protagonist goes on a quest to recover history of European ancestors: Jonathan Safran Foer. A secret world of masculine (and suspect) exhibition: Chuck Palahniuk. I could—I *will*—go even further and note that the whole underground breakdancing ring with neo-Nazi elements sounds like you put *Fight Club* and *American History X* in a blender. The play between hypertechnical and folksy speech (it's there in the novel—believe me) reads like a rip-off of David Foster Wallace. (And the chummy parenthetical asides are really just the cherry on top of that sundae of literary theft.) And the whole idea of a protagonist navigating a Rube Goldberg-style conspiracy, full of madcap conflations and charged with breakneck energy—well, that's everyone from Gaddis to Pynchon to DeLillo to Wallace.

Now, all those things are pretty cool when they do it. But, when I do it, it's a total disaster. It's like when I wear a tight flannel shirt buttoned all the way up to the neck: I'm neither one of the original hipsters nor an Armani model who takes the hipster to titanic, idealized heights. No, I'm just some poseur schlub who's mimicking what came before him.

I'm used to failing. My twenties have taught me all about failure in all its different varieties. When I went off to college in New York at eighteen, I thought I had MADE IT. Here I would be in the big city where all the cool kids were, and I could explode like a supernova. Eventually, I realized I had just the dim glow of a BIC lighter. An email account full of rejection slips and alerts for student-loan payments seems to be all I've earned for seven years of aspiration, striving, and frustration.

Well, I also have the bloody limbs of the novel I will never write. And why can't I write that novel—why can't I cross the line from golden aspiration to mediocre reality?

Good question. It's there in my parents' eyes when they see me come up from the basement for a smoke. "What's holding you back?" my sister asked me once. "It's just like a page a day for a year. Even I could do that." Of course, my sister goes to maybe the top law school in the country, so she doesn't understand how there can be such a gap between want and will. *You want to do it—just do it.*

But, when I face the novel I will never write, it's like a no-holds-barred wrestling match. Worst of all, that match features Me vs. Me. The decisions about the words on the screen force me into a trial where everything is up for grabs: what I think is good, what I think I am, what I think I want to be...you know the drill. *This paragraph totally sucks. No, this whole chapter sucks! No, I suck—suckety suck suck. (And you anonymous intern at* log x *who just rejected my fifteenth story—well, you suck, too.) The second face-off in the mall garage is crucial. It shows our hero's ability to face new challenges and hints at his vulnerability. No, I've already showed that before (see Chapter Four). So what does this face-off really add? It fills up pages but—what the hell, just cut it. But I love that paragraph! Make up your mind, Cohen. Well, nothing's wrong with weighing your words. I mean, Flaubert could spend hours just thinking of a sentence. Oh, the old Flaubert defense! SHUT UP SHUT UP SHUT UP.*

No wonder some days I barely make it to the end of a paragraph before I want to quit. No wonder many other days I choose weed and Wii over that despicable wrestling match. And the thing is, I don't know if this agony is even making it any better. It's like in my fiction workshops in college: some stories would get *so* workshopped and obsessed over. And you'd get three really incisive critique letters—*keep writing, keep writing, keep writing*—and you'd keep writing, but, after all those hours, you'd end up with something that was different from what you started with but not really any better.

Maybe that's a skill you need as a writer—to leap heedless and reckless over the abyss of despair. Or to have conviction, or something, despite the incessant rain of imperfection. Or maybe you need to be so swaddled in delusions that you can work in glad ignorance.

But I feel the rain, and I'm no good at jumping. Through a gap in the wrappings of my delusions, I see my mediocrity like a pulsing beacon. So I just struggle and despair.

Of course, that's pretty narcissistic for me to talk about my *struggle and despair*. Compared to most of the world, I'm Mr. Privilege. I've never had dysentery or seen a warlord's troops behead my dad or worked a 14-hour day in a sweatshop. You need a microscope to see how my pains actually matter.

One hungover afternoon, I calculated exactly how many more hours a day—a month—a year—I could have if I didn't have to face the novel I will never write. The calculation was more complicated than you might think. Not only did I have to account for the hours I spent struggling at the keyboard; I also had to include at least a portion of all the hours when I regretted doing something other than struggling at the keyboard, when I sat or smoked in a funk in dejection after struggling, when I stood like a mime at a party while thinking about some impossible passage, when I read other people's books in order to learn how to improve the novel I will never write, when I pestered my friends to read drafts, and so on. It was a lot of hours. I could have a life—like a whole life—if I stopped the insanity.

Sometimes, I think about giving up on the novel I will never write. If I did that, I would suddenly own my brain again. In place of the fictional colonies, I could have the wild pastures of happiness, excitement, and interest. Maybe I could take up a hobby—even exercising—something health-inducing and positive. Maybe I could commit myself to a real job and become, well, *respectable*. Maybe I could just stop the agony and give it all up. I wouldn't even have to do anything. I could just be free not doing anything. I could just bury those limbs, and let the earth devour them. Do you know how incredible it would be to never have to go into the basement again—to leave the wrestling mat for good—to stop picking at the scab?

I entertain that bold new plan, like a holiday in my head. But the holiday always ends. So I pick at the scab and squat before the mat and go down into the depths to work, once more, on the novel I will never write.

Chronically

by *Diannely Antigua*

It started when I was 16,
after instead of falling in love
with Jesus, I fell in love with a boy,
a little bit of God's wrath now living
in my right shoulder, right hip,
right side of my newly kissed neck.
I knew he was jealous,
God, not the boy. Maybe because
instead of reading a chapter in Proverbs before bed
I spoke to the boy on the phone, whispering, my body
cramped in the dark corner of the living room,
my family already asleep.
I told the boy I loved him, like a breathy hallelujah,
like the hush of the MRI machine, taking me
into its mouth, or the X-rays, or my silent
bending over in the blue paper gown,
little ass out in front of the doctor
as he checked my spine. And the boy
touched my spine too, as he reached under my shirt
unhooked my padded bra. This was before
the diagnosis, the word itself sounding like a disease,
diagnosis, how it shares the first three letters
of my name. *Diagnosis*. If I could take
my tiny shovel hand, carve out
the synapses from my head,
shoulders, knees and toes. O bless,
bless, bless, it is meaningless how invisible
the body in pain, when God
is a house I can't leave.

Get Off My Lawn
by Tanya Larkin

The yell that arose
from the shallow grave at the base of my brain
to interrupt my son as he reached
for the late lone tulip—
death-vaunting goth girl
queening the night in the middle of the day—
did not mark my best moment.

How could he know that dandelions were okay
to pick but tulips not? Not lilac branches
weighed down by their blooms
or a cascade of wisteria he could have used
as a shield against his enemies
who might have charged him and died
fake deaths en masse in the infinite
unfolding arms of its perfume.

Operation Wisteria Hysteria.
I prevented this. I who love
when children play dead and stare blankly
up, slack-jawed like the real dead
the one sky in each of their mouths
as they take turns on the ground.

Close my eyes! Close my eyes
with your thumbs. The dead say
to their friends who are busy

TANYA LARKIN

running around with clutches of grass
or waving whole pine saplings from afar
to toss upon the chests of their dead
before they stop short over the body
bowing their heads to intone
some sacred nonsense before subsiding
into silence the dead one can't bear
for long. She gets up and walks off
to a beckoning swing.
And the rest of them follow.

This is called starting a religion.
So unlike what happens at preschool
where the teacher turns off the lights
locks the door and tugs the blinds shut.
Behind the shelves, behind the cubbies.
Be silent, still. Like a rock, she says,
while the intercom bleats, this is only a drill.

My child, my child—he could have told you
that was a perfect, dead-on rhyme, but he wasn't
a very good rock. His leg shot out
from under him. He giggled and was shushed.
You could have asked him to be anything else!
A frog waiting for a fly, a gnome
charged with trapping an ogre.
Or just said the magic words:
camouflagereverse ambush predation.
He would have taken the game more seriously.

The way he might have done on the playground
I-mean-battlefield, in-the-house I-mean-outer-space

| 21

had his mother not tried to teach him
the finer points of civilization.
That we take care of a thing someone's cared for
by caring for that thing they have cared for
as I have cared for you and would hope
any stranger would let you live

so you could play dead and rise up
through the candied air of a different country
letting the flowers your mother told you
not to pick—those button-nosed roses,
that floppy poppy, those frowning
violets and tall purple afroed ones
no one knows the name of—
fall down your front and stream off your sides
leaving an outline of sticks and petals.

My Nature
by Tanya Larkin

You gave me your wildest no.
Thank you, I said.
I will keep it forever.
I will put it in a little box
and carry it across rivers
on top of my head
at daybreak.

I will bury it and dig it up
Bury it and dig it up.
Take it for a walk on the path
ignoring the rolling of eyes.

I had big plans for your no.
But it was so wild
I had to tame it first.
I said no to the no.
I told it to go to its room
or else.

Where it grew into a wilderness
which threatened to kill me
if I didn't enter it.
In this wilderness
the only defense
was defenselessness.

Go to your room, it said, or else.
So I went.
And found many rooms.
Every form of death
to lie down in and get up from—
refreshed.

At first I felt sorry for my name.
How it was always drowning
in your mouth. Code for
"I'm going under."

Then I realized I could always try
to have you. And that
could be a joke between us.

Isn't it always funny
to see a knight visor-down
swiping at trees in a wood
shaggy hemlocks in the tart air?

(What a fool—)
and yet it seems wise
to align oneself with no.
The word that will survive
all other words.

When I say it I get
a strong sense of déjà vu.
As if I am flowering in a copse.
Or have already become
the leaves some knight

is now slicing through.

I imagine myself alone
but in pieces. Companionable.
Golden flakes shuttering
all the way to the ground.
Not lonely at all.

What I could do with your no.
It is a gift so precious
so precious, I cannot accept it.

Lamplight on the River

by Shanti Thirumalai

I unfolded the fading black and red *dhurrie* on the floor and placed my sitar on it. My grandmother shuffled to the sofa, sat and picked up one foot and folded it under the other thigh. I brought her a cup of tea that was already beginning to cool, a film of cream rising to the top. I turned the ceiling fan off.

She blew on her tea. "Gita, I must come with you to Benares."

"Aji, I'd take you if I could." I was to leave the next day for Benares to attend a cultural meeting for medical students, where I was to play in a music competition. I was without doubt the best sitar player in my medical college, which was saying nothing at all. I had told Aji more than once that I couldn't take her, but she hadn't stopped asking.

"So why can't you?"

"I'll travel in a second class compartment, and sleep on the floor in some student hostel."

Aji stared quietly at her feet. "You do know why I want to go to Benares?"

"No," I said, not daring to guess. Aji's mind was ruled more by obsessions than by ideas. I wiped the sweat off my face with the free edge of my grey cotton *dupatta*.

"Before I die, I must free Ajoba's soul."

Every time Aji remembered Ajoba, my late grandfather, she would lapse back into another time, grieving a life she hadn't known. "It wasn't as it should have been," she said. "If those who love us, leave us, abandon us, we can never be the same. Yet, somehow, we must live, we live, a different life. I believed for all these years that he would return. You know, we had nothing with us, and your father was only ten years old. It was too dangerous to take the train from Lahore. We rode in a bullock cart and the animals died. Then we walked, slowly, for days, with neither food nor water."

This was an old story that lost nothing in its retelling. Sometimes Aji would describe how they sold her jewelry, how vultures feasted until they were too fat to fly, how crows pecked away at corpses and carcasses alike.

"Lahore was once a civilized city," Aji went on. "Your father played outside the *ajaib ghar* on the *zam-zammah*, that cannon of polished brass....it shone like pure gold. Then came the madness, farmers sold their live-stock, burned their fields of wheat. We lived through that, we made it to Hindustan. Then, one day, Ajoba went away." She clicked her fingers. "Not long after independence. Just like that, he was gone."

I wished I could take Aji's pain away. What then would she have left? Moth-eaten memory without pain? Dry brittle sorrow without tears?

Aji dabbed her eyes. "He could still be alive, somewhere, an old man. No, he would have found me. I can't imagine that he could be dead. I have fasted and prayed. He must have died, who knows when, or where, or by whose hand. So many years have passed. For my sake, perform the rites for Ajoba's soul." She straightened up as much as her bent and twisted frame would allow, radiant in her nine yard orange sari.

"Aji, why would you want to become a widow?" I asked. Aji clung to the privileges of the married woman, vermilion dot on her forehead, black and gold beaded necklace, green glass bangles. I did not want to ever see her forehead bare.

"I cannot let Ajoba's soul languish. You're too young, you couldn't understand. Ajoba immersed his own father's ashes in the Jhelum. As for your Ajoba, we never had ashes. Here, you have my authority, my permission, perform the rites, and let us be done with this business."

"As you say, Aji," I said.

"I've put this off for too long. Not a word to your father," Aji added in an unnecessary whisper. She had once, and only once, suggested to Apa that he fast on *ekadashi*, the night that follows the new moon, as a penance for souls of ancestors. Apa had erupted, decrying her irrational mind. He'd left in a rage, and my mother waited past midnight for him to stagger through the door.

I glanced at my watch. I hadn't decided which *raag* to play at the competition. "It's time for my practice. *Bhairav* or *Yaman*?"

"*Bhairav*," Aji said. "Ajoba's favorite, and perfect for Benares. We have a friend who lives there, a sitar player. What was his name? Your grandfather played *tabla* for him in Lahore. How they played, till two in the morning! All the neighborhood would listen, with windows open wide on cold nights to let the music in."

"I will play *Bhairav*," I said. I began to tune my sitar. "

"That is good, but first turn the fan on." Aji refused to believe that the rotating fan and moving air disturbed the tuning and undermined any resonance between string and wood. "Ravi Shankar doesn't care if the fan is on. He comes from Benares."

"When the fan is on, I don't sound like Ravi Shankar," I said. "I don't even sound like myself."

I began to play and Aji kept time imperfectly. Over the years I had developed a sense of rhythm that could withstand the enthusiasm of the amateur *tabla* player.

Maa and Apa came in an hour later, barely beating the traffic. Apa turned the TV on to watch cricket and I put my sitar away. The news in Marathi would be on at 7:30. Then all conversation would have to stop.

"Gita won't take me with her," said Aji. "Benares is a fine place to die. The soul is transported to Vaikunta. Those who desire nothing reach the realms of nirvana. That wouldn't be for me. I have too many desires."

"I don't want to go anywhere," Apa said. "Not Benaras and not Vaikunta. When I come home from work, I like to change into *dhoti-kurta*." That was not true. Apa often left after dinner to work on a play.

"I had a red sari from Benares, years ago. I'd love to get a new sari," Maa said. "Why don't you get me a sari? A blue one. Silk with *zari* on it. I'll give you the money." Apa never bought Maa anything, not even a sari for Diwali.

"Don't travel in the train with a sitar," Aji said.

"Borrow one," said Maa. "Or buy one."

"Why buy a sitar? You could easily borrow a sitar in Benares." Apa shook his head to agree with himself. "We knew a man who made sitars. He could play from his very soul. I heard Guruji play *raag Yaman Kalyan* in Pune twenty years ago. He told me after the concert that he still dreamed of my father."

"I told Gita about Guruji," Aji said. "Now, what was his name?"

"Devdutta Pandit. No, that's not it. Devavrata Pandit." Apa jabbed the air with his finger.

"The very man!" Aji said and clapped.

"Why do we drink tea on a hot day?" Maa said. "Put the fan on, Gita."

"He must be ninety years old," Apa said, tuning out the interruption. "Go see Professor Munshi at Benares Hindu University, Guruji's student. He might arrange for you to meet Guruji. Ask for a blessing!"

"Why ask for a blessing from another human?" said Maa. "He is not a God."

The fan groaned and came to life. "I would borrow a sitar," I said. "Preferably one that stays in tune when the fan runs."

"Guruji is from the Punjab *gharana*," Aji said. "But a true musician and a womanizer."

"The Punjab *gharana* isn't classical," Maa said.

"Allah Rakha, the *tabla* player and his son, what's his name, they are from Punjab *gharana*," Aji said. "Classical enough for me."

"Why does lineage even matter?" I asked.

"*Gharana* is everything," said Apa. "How can you have a tree without roots?"

The Benares Hindu University, despite its affiliation with Hinduism, did not support funeral ceremonies. In lieu of a rites and rituals office, there was a referral service. Pamphlets advertised religious solutions for funeral problems, immersion of ashes, and prayers for the recently dead, special prayers for those dead by unnatural means, accidents, murders, and suicides. Overdoses were doubly covered under suicide and accident. The rates were best, no bargaining, extra prayers at no additional cost with guaranteed everlasting peace for souls of beloveds.

I ran into Banashri, a classmate, at the desk. "I lost my father in an accident eight years ago. A car hit him. I saw him crumple and fall. *Hey Ram!*"

"*Hey Ram!*" I echoed. I hadn't known. Oh God. What did one say. After a long silence I said, "I need to perform rites for my grandfather."

"We could do this together," she said.

I doubted that our ancestors had met in any world but I was glad to have a friend in this one to negotiate with a priest.

I then made my way to the office of Professor Munshi of the North Indian strings section of the Department of Music. He wore a crumpled *khadi kurta* and his long white hair was unkempt. When I mentioned Guruji's name and explained my grandfather's relationship to him, he smiled and revealed a gap between his tea-stained teeth. "Guruji is living history, Father of Sitar, Pitramaha. I was his student," he said. He rang a bell and a woman brought two cups of steaming chai. "When Guruji came here after Partition, he was already a famous man. I've been a son to him yet there are days when he seems not to recognize me. Who knows if he will remember your grandfather!"

He switched on the ceiling fan and leaned back. The fan creaked, wobbled and swished into action, its yellowing blades black at the edges melding into a shade of grayish cream. The breeze unsettled the flies at the table.

"I seek his blessing," I said.

Professor Munshi smiled. "It's not often that I meet a student like you. Are you already a doctor?"

"Not yet," I said. "I will specialize in obstetrics."

"A lady doctor!" Professor Munshi said. "You'll bring babies safely into the world. When will you play sitar? Babies are born at inconvenient hours."

"Sitar was a hobby when I started," I said. "Now I don't begin my day without playing, if only for fifteen minutes. I can then ignore the stress of the suction machine that doesn't work or the patient who won't listen."

"You sound like a *bhairagi*, seeking, what.... equanimity? Eyes red from opium, happily indifferent. Music does not make one content or complacent. It sows dissatisfaction, a hunger, a thirst that is not quenched." Professor Munshi poured his tea into the saucer and slurped. "You need to transcend yourself, so Guruji says. Tell me now, how can I help you?"

"I need to borrow a sitar for the competition."

"That's easy," he said. "We have several fine instruments in the department."

"Thank you. There's something else, not related to music," I said. "I need to find a priest to help me perform rites for my grandfather."

"That's not unusual," he said. "Everyone who comes to Benares shares that same errand. I'll phone Munnaji, our taxi driver. He knows the priest."

Prof Munshi dialed a number, spoke in a low voice for a few minutes and turned to me. "The priest will be waiting at seven tomorrow morning at the steps to the river. Be ready to leave your hostel at six. Munnaji will be there. In the evening, he could bring you to Guruji's home, say at five. I'm not sure Guruji will see you though. He stopped allowing visitors four years ago after he broke his hip. If he doesn't ask you to sit, you must leave."

Munnaji, the taxi driver, was a well-fed man with oily black hair that stained the collar of his white shirt. He arrived at our hostel early the next morning in a black Ambassador. The sky was still the color of a dark pearl when we drove through the city. The ragpickers were already picking up cardboard and plastic; milkmen bicycled with their cylindrical pails of aluminum strapped on either side; men pushed handcarts holding blocks of ice insulated by jute and sawdust.

Munnaji parked the taxi at the entrance to the inner city, and introduced us to the priest. PappuLal Pandey wore an off-white *kurta* and *dhoti* and a large red *tilak* on his forehead, which established him as a religious-businessman. His graying hair was combed over a large bald spot and his gold-rimmed glasses briefly reminded me of Gandhi. PappuLal demanded money immediately, ostensibly for flowers and baskets.

I reached into my purse when Banashri put her hand over my wrist to stop me. She said to him, "Get whatever you need, we'll pay later when we return to shore."

PappuLal sniffed and walked ahead with Munnaji. We followed the men down an alley crowded with walls that leaned into each other. We deposited our slippers at a little shop and walked up to the wide riverfront at the Dasashwamedh *ghat*.

Munnaji hailed our boatman, Harish, who waited with his oars at rest. Despite the horizontal stripe of ash on his forehead, he had the look of a villain in a Hindi movie because of his black mustache that spilled over his cheeks.

The mist was thick and we could not see the other bank of the Ganga. Harish rowed effortlessly, and changed direction midstream with no obvious cue. We were surrounded by an envelope of white air, no north or south, no east, no rising sun in sight. He told us that his father, as his father before him, ferried pilgrims across the river. Times had changed, and Harish had also a job at an office. Floating past our boat was a tiny lamp of baked terracotta containing a little oil and a wick of cotton, its brave flame surviving the wake. The river flowed gently in her own time, dragging along a few stray garlands of marigold.

PappuLal told us that he was descended from a long line of priests, and the only one of his generation to follow the family tradition. His children would not become priests. "There could come a time," he said, "when there will be no priests to perform rites. What will become of souls then? Would they wander endlessly?"

I kept my eyes on the river, and wondered why the souls of the dead depended on skeptical grandchildren for salvation. We reached the other bank at a shallow area reserved for bathing and cordoned by stakes of metal and ropes of coir. There were a few men dipping in the water, heads under for a few seconds. "Leave your bags in the boat," the priest said. "*Jahaan dharm hey, wahaan paap hey.*" Where there is dharma, there is also sin.

Banashri stepped into the mud and held a hand out. I hesitated and clumsily swung myself into the shallows. The water was warm for November. We walked together into the marked area, holding hands to support each other. Banashri dipped twice and said, "I promised my mother I'd do this for my father. I have five brothers she couldn't be bothered to ask."

I loosened my hair and dipped in my turn. The water lapped over my ears. I went under with eyes open. Little black fish swam between the strands of my hair. I thought of my lost grandfather, stuff of legend, a freedom fighter, now finally dead to Aji. I barely believed half of what she said about him. I dipped for the death of filial love for my biological parents, surrendering that first abandonment, they were people who had never really existed. I dipped again for dead love, for the man I'd dared to love, who so quickly forgot me. Ganga, primal mother, I chanted, wash me pure, drown my sadness. I lingered with my head below the surface till Banashri tapped my shoulder.

We emerged from the water, took our clothes from the moored boat, and entered a changing area open to the sky, with screens of saris suspended between poles of bamboo tethered with ropes of coir and nylon. The sun appeared through the mist looking like the moon. We wiped away the sacred water, changed into dry clothes, and returned to the boat.

PappuLal had spread a thick sheet over the baseboards of the boat, and arranged two separate trays. We slipped on rings fashioned from blades of dried *kusa* grass to mark the beginning of the ceremony. PappuLal dipped a clay pot into the water and poured a little on each mound of wheat flour. "This was normally a man's job but these days so many women perform rites," he said. "I have come to accept that. Now, bind the flour firmly as you would *atta* for *chapatti*. Make three large balls and three small ones. Each ball represents a dead person. We pray only for the dead, and we pray only for those related by blood or marriage."

My prayers might do nothing for the soul of a man, who, for all I knew, might still be alive. We arranged the lumps of dough on a leaf, and decorated each lump with burnt rice, sesame seeds, sugar, flowers, turmeric and vermillion powder. PappuLal did not hold with silent prayer or meditation. He had us repeat after him the names of the principal beneficiaries, the family names, the stars they were born under to ensure that the merit of the ceremony was credited to the appropriate accounts. For Banashri's father, he said an additional prayer, a traumatic death merited extensive healing. He poured Ganga water three times into our open palms to drink. I swallowed the water as instructed before I realized what I was doing. The river carried waste of every sort, with the admixture of half-burned corpses. I faced the prospect of a life-threatening illness and found little comfort in the promise of instant nirvana.

"The prayers are over," PappuLal said. We released our leaves with decorated dough and flowers into the water, and watched them float away and disappear. "Feed a poor Brahmin to satisfy the soul. Would you like to pay for a year's satisfaction? Or five? As we say in Benares, there is no limit to generosity."

"I thought the soul would be liberated forever," I said

"Liberated, yes, but not fed," PappuLal said.

"I said we would pay for the service," Banashri said. "You want more money?"

"Only if you want to feed the soul."

"We shall feed orphans," Banashri said. "We were lost in the *puja* until you talked about money."

"There is no need for anger," PappuLal said. "Give only as much as you please. As for orphans, feed them by all means, but never let the souls of the dead want."

Munnaji and Harish, who were chewing *paan*, betel leaf and nut, returned to the boat, and we pushed off for the home shore. *Paan* made for the kind of bliss that cud-chewing cows enjoyed, but the *paan*-chewing man lost some of his dignity when he spat. Munnaji spat the blood-red remnants of his *paan* into the water. The stain spread and vanished. Where there is *paan*, there must be spitting.

"I would have tipped the priest if he hadn't asked," Banashri muttered.

How would giving PappuLal money be good for a dead man's soul? I wanted to believe in something, the goodness of the river perhaps. I was restless, agitated from hearing a priest and a supplicant squabble, greed meeting grief, leaving nothing, not even a sense of accomplishment.

"Benares is best seen from the river," Harish said when we returned to the *ghat*. "We could come back at dusk for the *aarti*, when you can listen to the singing and watch the lighting of lamps. And I can take you by motor boat to *Assi Ghat* where Maa Durga threw down her sword, exhausted as she was from fighting two demons."

Durga! I would play *raag Durga* in concert. It was a *raag* I had practiced for years, one I could play in my sleep. Durga was the mother of all the Gods, a creature of light. She decapitated demons and vanquished evil. I envied her power and her courage. As a

36 |

child I had been terrified of her open mouth that dripped blood into an empty skull.

Munnaji dropped us back with a promise to pick me up later in the afternoon to visit Guruji. I left the car feeling suddenly tired, wiped out. A gurgling in my stomach and a little cramp in my belly that followed soon reduced me to a creature of bowel and flesh. I spent the better part of the day in the lavatory, the squatting kind, before I ended the flux with pectokaolin that Banashri supplied.

"Ganga water is holy, not clean," she said. "You have been purged of your sins and sorrows! You have acquired not only merit but immunity to several waterborne diseases."

I had a bucket bath with tepid water and wore a pale green Calcutta silk sari. It was the color of raw coffee seeds, with a magenta border and I knew I looked good in it. Munnaji drove me through small streets, stopping for trucks, honking at buffaloes, cyclists, and even at a funeral procession. He would look for me in an hour, he said with a shrug, and added that waiting charges were not included. I shrugged back. I wouldn't pay him to wait. I walked through winding streets too narrow for the better-fed elephant, past flower sellers, and got barked at by a street dog.

It was almost five when I stood at Guruji's door. The electric bell at the entrance had been partially eviscerated. Red and black wires, possibly live, dangled at the switch to electrocute the unwelcome visitor. I knocked. A man with white hair reddened with henna answered. "What do you want?"

"I have come to see Guruji..."

A voice called from within. "Ask if she is the doctor."

"Are you a doctor?"

"Yes. I was told to come here."

Professor Munshi came to the door. "Your good name again, please? I forgot!" He was still in the same *kurta* and *dhoti*, more creased if that were possible.

"Gita. Gita Ranade."

"Yes! Guruji will see you." Professor Munshi opened the door wider to let me into a dark living room.

Guruji sat in a reclining chair, his feet propped up on a stool and covered with a dark woolen blanket. He had bushy eyebrows, long hair and a white beard. "You may sit down," he said after appraising me.

Bending over his footstool, I extended my arms, closed my eyes and touched his feet. A surge of veneration swept over me. "May I have a blessing?"

"You have all the blessings I can give," the old man said, flapping his hands in a shower of benedictions.

"My grandmother asked me to see you. My grandfather played *tabla* back in Lahore."

"I don't hear well. Speak up." He did not shout.

"Back in Lahore, my grandfather played *tabla* for you. *Tabla*." I mimed with my hands in the air.

"*Tabla* is not a musical instrument," he said.

"My grandfather was your friend." I repeated his name and saw no recognition.

"I had many friends, most of them are dead. I've lived too long. Last year I broke my hip." He looked at Professor Munshi as if to confirm, and stared pointedly at the servant. "Get us a drink, it is past five. Chai for the lady, she is not a drinking woman."

Turning to me, Guruji said, "Do you play *tabla*?"

"No, I play sitar."

"Good, I also play sitar, we have that in common. I made sitars that could sing."

His drink arrived, a tall silver tumbler half filled with whiskey watered down with ice. He took a sip and said, "Less ice and more whiskey, please. What have you given me? Only Munshi would drink this!" He returned the glass to the plastic tray the manservant held in front of him. "Munshi, didn't you say that a doctor was coming to see me?"

Professor Munshi put down his glass in a hurry, wiped his hands on his kurta and put his palms together. "She is a doctor and she plays sitar."

"Both!" the old man said and snorted. He cleared his throat and spat into a small cup that magically appeared before his mouth. The manservant put the spitting cup away and put the whiskey glass back in Guruji's hand. The drink looked as it did when first presented, no darker. "I have spent a lifetime doing just the one. What kind of doctor are you?"

Before I could reply, he turned to the manservant who returned with *chai* for me. "Close the windows before they start the *aarti*. Torture for one who loves music."

"Do you like the tea?" Prof Munshi said.

"Something to eat with it?" Guruji asked. "Dharampal, what is his name?" He looked for the hapless servant lurking near the big window. "The doctor will take biscuits with her tea."

The manservant shook his head and said, "We don't have any. You said we weren't to serve biscuits."

"Munshi!" Guruji said. "This doctor is our guest. Bring her some *rossogollas*. Make sure they're fresh. Last week someone got me a can of *rossogollas*. *Rossogollas* in a can! What will they think of next?"

Professor Munshi left without looking at me, and the door shut behind him.

"Your last name is Ranade?" Guruji said. "Shall we speak in Marathi? You will save some lives, and kill those you fail, *haan*?

What will happen, Doctor, when I die? All this talk of rebirth and heaven. Stories, for children. People are afraid to die. What do you think?"

I hesitated for a minute and said, "There is nothing ahead. Ashes...it's all here. In this one life." I blurted my truth, free not to pretend to believe in an afterlife.

"No one should live this long. I can't go to the bathroom on my own. Now if a cow were in my position, old, broken hip, they'd sell it to the butcher for bones. Make something with the hide." Guruji continued to mutter, half to himself, "Why should I go on? My bones hurt, and not just the ones I broke. Why doesn't Yama come?"

I tried to look professionally calm while I wondered what to say. Yama plucked away indiscriminately at young lives and hadn't found his way to the hearth of one so ready to die.

"We live as long as God wills." I repeated a platitude often used to placate relatives of sick patients.

Guruji raised his voice. "There are two secrets to a long life: Whiskey every day. From a silver tumbler. I only use Ganga water in my whiskey. Dharampal boils the water, even when I tell him not to. It's essentially pure even if it doesn't look like it. If you took the dirt away, it would be pure. Like the soul.

"The second secret," He said, dropping his voice and forcing me to strain my ears and lean forward. "The second secret is celibacy. I promised my father. I could never break that vow. I have been tempted, you know that man is merely an animal with clothes. Celibacy without the whiskey doesn't work. Whiskey by itself is just as useless. Do they teach you that?"

I nodded, wondering how I could escape. There was nothing to be had.

"I sleep on arrows, my back hurts," Guruji went on. "When can I return to my mother? My body cremated, ashes in the river."

Professor Munshi returned to the living room, his arms weighed down by brown paper packages containing sweets.

"Munshi, where did you go? Pull out a sitar! The one on the far left would be good for a woman. The doctor will play for us."

Professor Munshi opened a cupboard and brought a sitar to a threadbare red rug on the floor. He placed it beside Guruji's chair.

What would you like to play?" Guruji asked.

"May I play *raag durga*?" I said.

"Yes, *durga* is good at any hour." Guruji leaned his head into its long neck, and plucked the strings and tuned.

I sat cross-legged on the rug and picked up the sitar.

"Stop!" Guruji shouted. "The sitar is an object of worship."

I put it back down, touched it with the first two fingers of my right hand, touched my eyes with those fingers and lowered my eyes. Guruji grunted.

I checked the tuning; it was perfect.

"You found the tuning satisfactory?" Guruji said. "I checked the strings myself."

I lowered my eyes again and said, "May I play?"

"In a minute. When you play *durga*, or any *audawa raga*," Guruji said, "try and think of a stream of melting snow rushing down a mountain slope. There are five boulders to help you get across. You have to be sure-footed and strong, or you could be swept away. Which *tal*?"

"*Rupak*?"

"*Rupak!* Seven beats......yes. Munshi, you think *rupak*?"

"More interesting than *teen tal*," Professor Munshi mumbled. He had rediscovered his whiskey and appeared to be talking to it.

I plucked the strings softly, unsure of myself.

"Wait!" Guruji said. "Come closer. I can feel better than I can hear."

I moved closer to Guruji and turned to let him touch the high end of the instrument with his right hand. Its base was big and heavy with a neck no wider than my own sitar at home. There was nothing ornate about it, yet its sound was deeper, richer, more resonant than any sitar I'd ever heard.

"Let me hear you play the scale. You know the notes?"

It was a lot harder than I expected. I tried to please a cranky old man with impossible standards.

"Easy on *dha*, gentle, let it slide from *sa*, and hold it," Guruji said. "*Ma* and *re* don't move a hair. Not *shuddha saveri*! Less passion, more control. Play!"

I played the *alap* slowly. I moved to *jor alap* once I got used to the instrument, and Professor Munshi kept time with his hands. I finally picked up the pace, closing my eyes to hear. I played better than I could, and soon I was unaware of the room, unaware of Guruji. I stopped hearing the music, stopped feeling the strings. I stopped being Gita, I surrendered to Maa Durga. She found a sense of cold purpose, ruthless drive, she summoned strength and fought fear and fatigue. She mustered fury and restrained it, wielded the sitar like a sword, a touch, a thrust, assaults on evil forces, emotions stilled. I opened my eyes to see Guruji's face wet with tears. "You brought Durga Mata here," Guruji said. "Now, summon Yama if you will. And let me wish this for you: May all your desires be fulfilled, and may all your desires be worthy of fulfillment."

I stood up and folded my palms, lowered my head till it reached my hands.

"Let me give you another blessing: immortality. Something you'll want until you grow so old. I will die soon. So I've decided," Guruji said. "I will recite the thousand names of God, for Munshi, for Dharampal, that they may hear.

"I've never forgotten you," he shouted suddenly, glaring at me. "I know why you're back! You've returned to kill me." He dropped his voice. "Forgive me, I made a terrible mistake, it was another life. A foolish old man begs forgiveness." He reached out and grabbed my wrist and squeezed it.

"I would never hurt you," I said, trying to pacify him. How could I ease his suffering, bring him a modicum of solace? What did one do for the living?

Guruji looked at me, calmer, his eyes filled with sadness, regret. "Ganga has forgotten her son. I ask you for a favor. Go, send a lamp down the river, ask my mother to take me back." His voice petered out and the *aarti* began at the *ghat* and filled the room with booming sounds of drums and cymbals.

I held his hands, kissed his fingers and picked up my bag.

"I suffer the *aarti* every evening," Guruji said. "Even with the windows closed, I hear every false note. I should take off my hearing aids." His fingers fumbled and an earpiece fell onto his chair, rolling into the recesses of overstuffed cushions.

Professor Munshi saw me out.

"I will need a sitar for the competition tomorrow," I reminded him.

"I haven't forgotten."

I walked into the crowd at the *ghat* to watch the last of the evening prayers, the *aarti*, where priests held large oil lamps while dancing in white *dhotis* and bare chests with only the sacred thread worn over a shoulder. *Om jaye jagdisha hare*. The well-worn tune inspired uncommon courage in the lay person who joined in the singing.

Harish the boatman stood at the edge of the crowd, where he chewed *paan* with Munnaji. "Let's go to *Assi ghat* before it gets dark. My boat is ready."

"Let me buy a lamp first." I picked up a small lamp half-filled with oil with a cotton wick from a wayside stall. The shop keeper lit it with a match.

We rowed past a series of *ghats* descending from crumbling mansions on the riverfront. Pilgrims were bathing, men were washing clothes in the fading light. The milkmen rinsed their cylindrical pails in the same water. An empty coconut shell bobbed past. We turned around at *Assi ghat* and headed to *Rajghat* on the Southeast end, past *Manikarnika ghat* where people waited to die. I counted seven burning pyres, stony grief carved on the faces of mourners. Shiva was there, and Yama, and the name of Rama was the truth. There was no higher virtue than Truth. So it had always been, so it would be forever.

I sent the lamp of red clay with its little flame into the Ganga with a prayer: Mother, bring your son home.

We passed a bloated corpse in the water, very dead, skin macerated and white. "Which way does the river flow?" I shuddered.

"East," Harish said pointing. "You bathed upstream, on the other shore."

"I know a good sari shop, fair in price," Munnaji said when we reached the steps. I was sure he worked for commission. "The car is parked close to it."

"Let's go there now." I picked a peacock blue sari for my mother, dark silk accented with threads of green and purple and gold.

Professor Munshi sent for me the next morning to lend me his own sitar, one Guruji had made. He escorted me to the hall and sat in the center of the first row. The audience was restless and showed no signs of settling down. I could barely hear myself play with the ambient noise, and I could not lose myself. I tried to go back to Guruji's living room and play as I played for him. Nothing. I had nothing to give. The clean notes sounded mechanical as I traversed the scale, easy on the *dha, ma* and *re* moving not a hair. I nodded to signal a stop; the *tabla* player, a solid accompanist, nodded back, waited a split second and ended with a quick flourish.

An hour later, I collected first prize feeling hollow. I said to Professor Munshi, "I played better yesterday."

"You were not inspired today," he said. "You know intuitively what cannot be taught. Guruji has instructed me to give you the sitar you played on at his home. He said he'd been saving it for you. It was the last one he made. Munnaji will bring it in a case to the railway station."

Aji was alone when I returned home two days later. "Aji," I said, touching her shriveled feet, "Ajoba's soul is free. The priest, PappuLal, ate well for Ajoba."

Aji smiled. "That was a good thing you did, sheer *punya*. You have come home with a sitar, I see. You met our friend, the sitar player?"

"Guruji? Oh yes! He said he'd never known in his life a *tabla* player as good as Ajoba."

Aji clapped her hands. "They were such dear friends."

"He said you were the most beautiful woman in Lahore," I said, and added in a tone that invited confidences, "Was he in love with you?"

"Silly girl, you say such outrageous things. I remember a young woman who was in love with him but he was cruel to her," Aji said. "She died, I don't know why, and he never did marry."

"Guruji gave me a blessing with this sitar. And he said I shouldn't play with the fan on."

Aji laughed. "You just made that up. Did you buy your mother a sari?"

"Of course," I said. "Let me show you."

"Later. After you've eaten. I dreamed of you. In my dream you were sick and I prayed for you to recover."

Aji slipped off her bangles and her *mangal sutra* of black beads. She was free at last from the oppressive weight of the shadow years without Ajoba. She smeared her *kumkum* with the back of her hand, pulling a red streak across her forehead. Then she began to sob, shocked awake and swept by rude waves of latent grief. "What has happened! I am now a widow. How will I ever bear such sorrow? Oh, Gita, I am so tired. I could sleep now and never wake up."

I wrapped my arms around her, rocking her gently until she was spent, and I waited quietly at her bedside until she fell asleep.

Find Everything You Are Looking For?

by Grace Segran

John appeared from the stationery section in Aisle 3 and shuffled towards me at Register 1, holding a greeting card with arthritic fingers.

"Good morning, John," I said as I reached out to take the card from him. "Only this today?" He smiled and said, "Yes" in a quiet raspy voice. As I turned over the card to scan it, I saw that the inside read: *To the woman I love. Thank you for being my wife.* I thought of 90 year-old Eli Wallach, who played the Arthur Abbott character to perfection in the movie *The Holiday*, as a man deeply in love with his wife.

"It's a Mother's Day card for my wife," John said, as he struggled to take out his wallet from the pocket of his crumpled jacket. Then he leaned toward me and whispered with a wink: "We've been married seventy-two years and she's still getting used to me."

It is moments like these that make my day as a "cashier of a certain age."

We were living in London when Raja, my husband of 31 years, died in 2011 as a result of open-heart surgery to replace an abnormal heart valve he was born with. Three years later, I decided to take a couple of years off from my full-time job as a journalist and editor to go back to school to study creative writing in the U.S. It was a means to an end: the student visa afforded me residence so that I could be near our daughter who was living in Cambridge, Massachusetts.

With a semester more to go, I started applying for jobs. After being rejected from thirty-six executive and fifty-eight administrative job applications in nine months, I decided it was time to try something different, if only to have something to do. By then, I had completed my degree and was in a stupor on the couch most days, paralyzed by the lack of purpose. I ate snacks rather than real food because it was less work. I watched two seasons of The Marvellous Mrs. Maisel in two days and reruns of other tv shows, and avoided the news channels because I didn't have the physical, mental and emotional stamina to engage the wretched political scene. A diabetic, the sedentary life caused my sugar to stay high and I had to increase my insulin intake to cope with the highs. Then I read about college graduates who'd applied for more than two hundred jobs and were reduced to sitting on sidewalks with signs advertising their skills. If twenty-two year-olds couldn't get jobs, what about sixty year-olds like me? Past my use-by date.

Despite the naysayers among my family and friends, I decided to see what was happening in retail. I'd always wanted to sell things when I was a kid. Must be the money—people hand over money to the seller. Who wouldn't want that? I finally got to live that dream when I was offered a cashier position at a nation-wide pharmacy close to home. I wasn't aiming for the big time; district manager or communication director were not possibilities for me, a latecomer in the retail space. The store wasn't a charming bookstore or a café where reporters and managing editors might like to languish between assignments. An associate position comes with the stigma of being at the bottom of the food chain: menial work with no authority, a thankless job. The working environment is not glamorous or prestigious. My daughter, also a journalist, was apprehensive about my working in retail. "Are you sure you want to do this, Mom? It's hard work and the management style is not what you are used to." "But I get to work the magical machine called a cash register," I said gleefully. So I swapped my trusty laptop for a touch screen device at the Point of Sale.

It takes me nineteen minutes to walk to work from home, in the direction of the hills just outside of Boston. A course that takes me past Victorian and Colonial houses on the left and the high school on the right, the popular public pool, the beloved town library, and the bustling post office—usually with a dog tied to the railing at its entrance—before I turn right, away from the hills through the commuter rail underpass to the store.

It has a townie feel to it. I see the same people coming in at the same times of the day. Ronald comes in at 8:30am for his coke, two cheese sticks, a bun or a small pack of biscuits. Then Lorna stops by just before 9:00am, plops her can of Red Bull on the counter before crossing the street to the liquor store where she works. Most Sunday evenings around 7:00pm, a 30-something father comes in with a toddler and preschooler and lets them loose. The toddler heads for the 10-shelf display of miniature cars by the photo section and takes them all for a spin. The preschooler kicks the beach ball around the store, while the father reads magazines in Aisle 4 undeterred by the commotion his kids are creating. Half an hour later, he buys a pack of chewing gum and departs unapologetically, leaving me to clear the debris throughout the store.

Still, I enjoy working the weekend evening shift. Evening is my favorite time of day. It's when nature changes her guard and the stars come out. It's the ending of another day and being thankful for it. This mood sets in acutely between 6:00pm and 8:30pm when

I am at the register. Families and couples drop by to pick up gum in the early evening or a tub of Ben and Jerry's to finish their evening at home. They have all come out to eat in our one-street town center with its disproportionately high number of restaurants, and my heart aches for Raja. I miss the time we spent together, going to our "local" on weekends. In Paris, where we lived for five years in the sixteenth arrondissement, it was the nondescript corner brasserie on Rue de la Pompe—a two-minute walk from our apartment, for the humble but exquisite *steak a point et un rouge*. We had two tours of duty in London and both times lived in Chiswick by the river. Our local was The Black Lion five minutes away by the Thames Path—he'd have the shepherd's pie and a pint, and I would have the Sunday roast. In Singapore where we lived in between tours of duty, we'd drive five minutes from our home to Changi Village and eat at a hawker center where we were spoilt for choice, and finish the day with a stroll on the beach. The memories are bittersweet and descend insidiously. *Saudade*. Portuguese for a deep nostalgic longing for someone who will not return. Inexplicably, I derive comfort from the warm, gentle sadness, a sweet walk into the past with Raja momentarily.

During my first week at work, I was taught "facing," which is the act of straightening the items so that the shelves look smart and welcoming. I enjoyed arranging the cereal or multivitamin boxes in a straight row, and moving the milk cartons forward as they were being sold. Walking through the aisles, I picked up "drop-off" items that were left throughout the store when customers changed their minds. I also learned to use the Symbol, a device made by a company called Zebra. It is the size of a cell phone and identifies products and manages inventory. In 2011, when I was covering the Bloomberg Businessweek European Leadership Forum in London, I interviewed Anders Gustafsson, CEO of Zebra, and learned about RFID and inventory. RFID takes information and puts it in an electronic format that makes the information versatile and accessible. This helps to automate and drive efficiencies in supply chain logistics. I was fascinated by the technology in the store. Is what I am doing RFID in action? I wanted to know more about how it actually works and the extent to what it could do. But my coworkers could only show me how to use the Symbol to find where the item was located.

The store's FM radio has an upbeat, addictive playlist that includes my favorite artists such as John Legend, Adele, Michael Bublé, and Carole King. I tap and sing along in my head to Elton John's "Crocodile Rock" as I insert new item labels for sunscreen in the seasonal aisle. The music makes work light and so much more fun. The DJ just needs to add in Ed Sheeran and it would be perfect.

I know my regular friendly customers by name. Barb was very kind and patient when I messed up her transaction during my first week; I always look forward to seeing her in the store when she brings her mom to do the weekly shop of chocolate and magazines and monthly hair color. Romeo owns the Italian cafe across the street and waits patiently in line to get change for his register or to get ice when he runs out. Late one busy evening, he sent over a large pizza with four different quarters of pies.

The acerbic ones approach my counter with a churlish tone before I even have a chance to greet them and ask: "Find everything you are looking for?" Interaction with these folks is guaranteed to be unpleasant and I often have to bite my tongue and smile like a fool because I'm on the wrong side of the cash register. In a predominantly white affluent town, it doesn't help that I am Asian with a non-American accent and communicating according to script, as though I had learned it on the boat coming to America. During training, my manager taught me this drill: Wish the customer "Good morning" when they come up to the register. Then ask "Do you have our Rewards card?" When I am completing the transaction, ask "Is there anything else I can help you with?" And then say "Thank you." After a month of working like a programmed robot and gaining confidence in my job, I decided I wanted to be human. That morning, a 35-ish woman in a red shift dress with a black Kate Spade work tote on her right arm, walked up to the counter.

"Good morning," I said.

"I don't need a bag," she said without making eye contact, as she pulled out her crisp striped Kate Spade wallet.

"Okay," I said. I scanned her Rewards card, followed by a mini can of Altoids and thinkThin chocolate mint protein bar. "Pity about what happened to Kate Spade."

"Yeah," she said. She stopped texting on her iPhone, encased in a candy-striped Kate Spade cover, and looked at me. "And also the other guy….uh…" she said, squinting her eyes, "I forget his name."

"Bourdain. Anthony Bourdain," I said. I hit CHARGE after she slotted her credit card into the machine.

"Yeah. Him. My mom loves his show. She's going to be so sad."

"Me too," I said as I handed her the receipt. "Have a good one."

"You too," she smiled at me. She dropped her purse and phone into her tote, took out her car keys, and turned towards the door.

I had totally deviated from company script and was afraid of being scolded for it in a place which did not seem to allow autonomy, but I felt I met—no, exceeded—the spirit of the Standard Operating Procedure: I had delivered good personalized customer service by engaging the customer who wanted to engage, while meeting their retail needs efficiently. And that must be good for business, I reasoned. More importantly, it felt human and organic. For some other customers, the company script is perfect, though I might sometimes add something personal. "Take care of that arm," I said to Mrs. Clarke who came in to get an arm sling after she fell the previous day.

I came to the job with no expectations. I had an idea of what it entailed, having been in many of its stores before but I never internalized what it would mean for me. I was at rock bottom, purposeless in my life, so I wanted to make this work. Work is physically demanding especially when it is busy. It's a small store and I am usually the only one on the floor, working the register and stocking the shelves when there are no lines. I move nonstop for the six or more hours during my shift. And I love it. I feel I am doing something meaningful—interacting with customers and serving them by walking them to the product they are looking for. Stocking the shelves helps to meet customers' needs. To me, stocking is like assembling a puzzle where I find the missing pieces and make it complete.

My favorite activity of all is when the truck comes in on Wednesday nights after the store closes. The young chaps from Ghana and Haiti unload the shipment. As we bring in two-wheel trolleys precariously stacked eight totes high and place them in specific locations throughout the store, I'm entranced by their accents and witty observations of daily life in a new country. They remind me of Brussels, Jakarta, Manila and all the places where I'd been a stranger in a strange land at their age—at once terrifying and exciting. Then we each take a section and start stocking the shelves till past midnight. It is wholly satisfying that I can concentrate on one task and see it through without being interrupted by the ping of the bell (again) at the counter when someone is ready to check out.

I enjoy being with my co-workers. I feel a sense of community as we share parenting and pet stories, exchange recipes, and commiserate over burst pipes in winter. However, sometimes I miss the repartees and exchange of ideas with fellow writers and editors, the satisfaction of problem solving and putting an issue to bed. I couldn't ask my co-worker, in between lines at the register, what she thought about Trump's latest conspiracy theory or Kavanaugh's nomination because she doesn't read or watch the news. My son-in-law, a political scientist at the Harvard Kennedy School, tells me my town votes Democrat but I suspect my white colleagues belong to the demographic group that seem to go overwhelmingly for Trump—some of them have never even been to Boston, only eight miles away. The twenty-somethings who work in the store do not know who Sandra Bullock ("Yes, I think I've heard of her…isn't she the one who acted in Mamma Mia?") or Ed Sheeran is ("Ed-shee who?"). Nor that *Ocean's Eight* is now playing in a theatre near us ("Is it the one about the boat?"). I always offer to put the day's newspapers on the stand in the morning so that I get to linger over the headlines on the top half of the folded *Boston Globe* and *The New York Times* while putting away *The Wall Street Journal* and *The Boston Herald*. During my fifteen-minute break, in between bites of low-carb cheese biscuit and gulps of bottled water, I try to scan the day's headlines on my phone or *The New Yorker,* if it has already come into my inbox. To get my fix of world news and life, I do a WhatsApp chat late into the night with my friend, Heather, who lives in Perth, Australia and is twelve hours ahead of me.

A month after starting work, my muscles attuned themselves to the new normal. I felt a sense of wellbeing. There was energy in my step. Initially, the constant walking and heavy lifting during each shift caused my blood sugar to drop and stay way below the normal level of 120mg/dL. A diabetic, I tried to bring the sugar up with glucose tablets that I had stuffed in my pockets, but without much success. My body was using it up extremely fast. My endocrinologist cut my basal insulin dose by one-third. The intense physical activity and losing three pounds in the first week alone had improved my body's sensitivity to insulin. I started cooking again—baking low carb snacks like coconut flour lemon cake and almond flour cheese biscuits for work and preparing meals, instead of lumbering to Burger King or the convenience store up the street.

Not only that, I had started writing and reading again. I wanted to do mundane things like weed out my books and papers that had gathered in piles the past year and reorganize the kitchen and basement—activities which felt to be too much for me when I didn't have a job. My days off were fun and enjoyable, whether I was reading in a café with my flat white and bacon sous vide, watching *Black Panther* or *The Incredibles 2* at the cinema, or taking the ferry to Martha's Vineyard. The quiescence had thawed and I regained my joie de vivre. Viktor Frankl, a psychiatrist and Holocaust survivor, was right after all. The primary purpose of life is the quest for meaning and is derived from three possible sources: purposeful work, love, and courage in the face of difficulty. Unexpectedly, in retail, I'd found everything I was looking for.

Appetite

by Kat Read

My husband Will told me that he once stood at the kitchen sink to eat a pig's foot. He had followed a recipe from his favorite cookbook, simmering a blend of sticky soy and orange and molasses and pig parts. For hours, the feet bobbed in the inky sauce alongside slices of pork belly. And when they were tender, he rolled up his sleeves and plucked a foot from the pot and took a bite, sauce dripping down his chin and into the bottom of the sink. Plink. Plink. He finished the whole thing.

    I wasn't there for the pig foot, but the image blooms in my mind. This is a man who hungers, who tastes, who can spend hours getting the sauce just so but, once it is, cannot wait for a plate.

    Will is always eating, often very strange things in very strange ways. Scarfing down pickled eggs straight from the jar with the fridge door still open, his face and bare arms bathed in eerie blue green light. Standing at the threshold of the kitchen, cradling a slice of pumpkin pie in the palm of his hand, the buttery crust greasing his skin. Smearing a cracker with creamy feta and topping that with a cube of cheddar and then a wedge of quince paste. Peeling open a cold cooked lobster and pulling the flesh from the shell with his fingers. He is trying, he is tasting, always, always.

We tend to think of passionate eaters as greedy, but that's never been true in my experience, and especially not with Will. The first time I visited him in his home city of Halifax, he took me for poutine at a college bar and I felt the curds squeak between my molars, lubricated by unctuous gravy. He drove me to Peggy's Cove, a beautiful historic fishing community outside of Halifax. Once we arrived, he insisted that I try herring with sour cream on a cracker and I winced with anticipatory disgust. The combination of cold pickled fish and cream was...not for me. When we got back to his apartment, we stood shoulder-to-shoulder in his tiny galley kitchen and he showed me how to break down a whole duck, snipping up the spine with kitchen shears. It made me feel confident, like a proper cook. We let the duck marinate in orange juice studded with whole cloves and star anise while we made basil simple syrup on the stove for daiquiris.

Will and I were just friends for more than ten years, often in relationships with other people. We met working at a summer camp, our fingers perpetually covered in the sticky remnants of toasted marshmallows. Before Will and I were married, I mostly dated men who didn't care much for elaborate meals or obsessing over food. I always felt deficient in relationships because I hungered too much. I wanted to go to that new wine bar across the street, I wanted to buy that whipped honey at the farmers' market, I wanted to stop for a waffle at the food cart parked outside the grocery store. "I could eat the same thing every day," one of my exes would often say, pride in his voice. It sounded like a statement of his moral steadfastness that stood in contrast with my wicked appetite.

I tried to make those relationships work and to suppress my desire to try new things. But I would inevitably end up on a food blog or paging through a cookbook at Kitchen Arts and Letters on the Upper East Side of Manhattan and I would start to salivate. So I would take out my phone and text Will, because Will got it. Food became the safe place for us to explore our unspoken love and desire for one another. When we were apart, we would post links on one another's Facebook walls, recipes for s'mores martinis and satirical articles about kale. And when we were together, we were always eating.

Of course, it was foolish to think we could connect over food and keep things platonic. Food is the least safe place when it comes to love and desire. To share a meal with someone is to share an experience of intense intimacy. What is on the plate becomes part of you, literally part of you, feeding your cells to fuel breath, heartbeat, senses. I would think about that when I ate with Will. Sitting across from him at a table brought into focus the edges of my body, the feel of my tongue in my mouth, my corporeality. I felt full--of food and of drink, and even though I had not yet admitted it to myself, of love.

Will would visit me about once a year when I was living in New York City and we would plan elaborate food adventures, trying to taste as much as possible before he would have to go back home to Halifax. On one visit, we couldn't decide where to have dinner, so he suggested that we make reservations at two different places. We started the evening at The NoMad, an elegant restaurant with exquisite food, sipping cocktails and sharing tagliatelle with meyer lemon and king crab. We were seated at a small table in the center of the room and every time one of their famous roast chickens came out of the kitchen, we were four blue eyes tracking it across the floor.

We had time to kill before our reservation at the French bistro Les Halles, so we stopped at an Italian market. We wandered around without a basket and I watched him fill his arms with packets of bresaola and prosciutto cotto and containers of olives and wedges of ricotta salata. He stacked them one on top of the other and I felt so giddy to know him. It was one of the best dates of my life, except for the small detail that we weren't dating.

On another of his visits to New York, we went to Le Bernardin, the legendary four-star French restaurant. We could only get a reservation for nearly eleven o'clock at night, but we dressed for prime time, Will in a beautiful jacket and tie and me in an embroidered dress and heels I could barely walk in. He ordered the tuna with foie gras and put his fork down after he took the first bite, his eyes filling with tears of joy because of what he had just tasted. Watching his vulnerable reaction felt so intimate. I placed my hand on his arm and smiled at him and we both knew that the staff believed we were a couple. We didn't correct them.

When we finally admitted our feelings for one another, it was two nights later at a hip Mexican restaurant with tin trays and paper napkins. We ate fish tacos with cabbage and cilantro and chipotle aioli. We were emboldened to speak by the margaritas we sipped out of mason jars, the heady tequila and the bitter lime, bitter as a life without one another would be. "I love you," he said, aioli greasing his lips, "And I always will." I looked at him across the table and years of denied appetite suddenly came roaring through. There was no question we would be together.

Since then, we have stopped at a small pushcart in Maine to slurp oysters while standing on the sidewalk, throwing the shells into a bucket. We have seared foie gras for dinner at home and served it with a smear of peanut butter and tangy cranberry jelly on brioche. We have sat on stools at Little Oak Bar, our favorite bar in Halifax, with our knees touching and our hands wrapped around negronis and ordered absolutely every bar snack on the menu.

We have stopped for coffee, and I have watched as he brings my iced coffee to the milk bar, no lid, almost overflowing. I have watched as he placed his lips to the brim and slurped until there's enough room in the cup. I have watched as he pours in cream, so much cream, probably too much cream, until it's just how I like it, and watched as he brings me the cup, an everyday act of extraordinary love.

After our wedding, we went out for lunch with our families at a quiet diner by the sea near my hometown in Massachusetts. We put my bouquet in a plastic mug on the table, a makeshift centerpiece for our little wedding reception. We poured hot butter over the lobster rolls until they glistened, shared eggplant fries, snuck fried clams off of my mom's plate. We were a tangle of arms and forks braiding into one another, angling to try all the different types of pie that we ordered. It was perfect.

Later that day, we drove to New York for our honeymoon, and we made reservations in advance to go back to The NoMad and Le Bernardin. Again, the food was remarkable, but it was even better to hold hands with him on top of the table.

Does the Name Blackie Donovan Mean Anything to You?

by Ron MacLean

There's this little guy on my porch I've never seen before. He's a caricature of an Irish thug and he's looking for Mikayla, my daughter, who he accuses of wronging his boss.

"Blackie Donovan doesn't forget," the guy says. He points across the street at the neighbor's shrub-guarded lawn. "He was out there an hour ago. He'll be out there tomorrow. He'll be out there until this is made right." With each statement, the guy flings his arm out at the shrubs anew, as if punctuating a threat. I'm trying to process the logic. Mikayla's eleven. How could she have run so afoul of someone? She's a good kid, works hard in school, supports herself with two jobs – she's always been independent. I'm staring down at the henchman. He's got black hair and acne and a reddish tint to his pasty white skin. A black leather jacket that reeks of nicotine. He's actor short and self-conscious. Probably nineteen. I'm about to tell him that I don't know what to tell him – she's on her own now, if he's got a beef he should take it up with her – when he shoots me a look, eyes hooded, lips pinched: "I'll be seeing you." And walks away.

"Does the name Blackie Donovan mean anything to you?"

My ex- is over for dinner. We hang out a lot – so much so that I can't remember why we split. She can.

"No," she says. "Should it?" She's addicted to my cooking. What I do with green chilies should be against the law. It makes her somewhat willing to discount my less endearing qualities. I tell her what happened the day before. As I do, I'm mulling possibilities for who this Blackie guy could be. Is he the kid in homeroom she busted for texting? Her sixth grade shop teacher, who she taunts because he never finished high school?

"What's that Mona's last name?" the ex- interjects.

I shrug. "You're thinking Mona's big brother?" Mona's the kid's colleague from the diner, who Mikayla thinks doesn't pull her weight on the job.

I'm looking at the kid's class picture, framed on my buffet. While she has her mother's cinnamon hair and soft green eyes, mostly she favors me: sharp-jawed, stubborn-faced. I eat. I ponder. "What about Scott Martin?"

"The one who stuck gum in her hair in second grade?" She sounds dubious. But how do we know? There are so many possibilities. Kids are kids, and our girl can be a little dramatic. I'm pondering whether this is a problem when the doorbell rings. I gesture, like *you get it, see for yourself*. She's reluctant, but it rings again and she, unlike me, can't leave a bell unanswered.

So it's the same henchman and he says the same stuff in his would-be tough guy voice. This time he adds, "Someone's gonna pay."

Back at the table, the ex- plays with her fork in the chili sauce. She's distracted. Disturbed. Peppers, polenta and melty cheese shift on her plate like unstable continents. I eyeball her *see, I told you*. "Did you set this up?" she says. "Is this your weird idea of a joke?" She's still semi-mad at me from the clown-school- dropout incident.

I shake my head. "It's like I told you."

"You think she really did something? Serious?"

"I'm wondering." I'm thinking about accountability, whether to go to bat for the kid, and if so how far. "I'll call the homeroom teacher. What's his name?"

"It's a her," the ex- says. "And no, you won't. Mikayla would be mortified."

I know. Mostly she makes good choices, our Mikayla. And when she doesn't we try to remember she is only eleven. But what about personal responsibility? Besides, we're her parents. We should model appropriate behavior. I eat a bite of chili. "She's too smart to get caught up. Isn't she?"

The ex: "Are we being fair? Maybe she's got a problem. Maybe it's a mistake." The lingering musk of nicotine-haunted leather infects our meal. "Did you call her?" Our daughter lives alone. We each do. It's easier. "Ask her if she knows any Blackie Doherty?"

"Donovan," I say. "And no. You ask her. She won't take me seriously." Could Blackie be her bookie? Maybe she's behind on the vig. Pulled a Pete Rose with her softball team. No. She's no gambler. Besides, she's great with finances. She's negotiating to buy the building she lives in.

The ex- calls her. The kid insists she's never heard of Blackie Donovan.

Two nights later we're at my parents' place, birthday dinner for my dad. I've had another visit from Blackie's man. Explained how it's a mistake, my daughter doesn't know the guy. He was having none of it. Next thing I knew, he's on tiptoes and my shirt was bunched in his fist. He was more powerful than I figured. Smoke breath in my face as he stage whispered what was supposed to be a threat: "Nice windows you got, but rock smashes scissors every time."

Anyway, my parents'. Mikayla is there – a rare night off – with the current boyfriend, a sixth grader whose name I don't remember. Brown curls and a hockey face – the wide frame, the thickness of purpose, the missing teeth. He's the tallest kid in school, but you can tell he's done growing and will be a stumpy adult in a way that's somehow, inexplicably, his fault. He could be someone's henchman himself.

Lamb meatballs over pasta with mom's gravy, same as every year.

I get there late. Everyone's seated, including the management team from my former company, some of whom I failed to fully compensate when I sold the business out from under them. I'm not happy to see them – the beards, the gingham shirts, helping themselves to my mother's cooking – and I'm about to say *Ma, why do you bring my enemies to your table* when the doorbell rings. Mom answers. It's the thug. I shoot the ex- a knowing look. The kid shrunk down in her seat like she doesn't want to be here. The boyfriend a hockey-faced blank page. The ex- kicks me under the table like *do something*, but I'm leaning left to make sure I can't be seen from the doorway. Who is this character and what's he really after? Is he acquainted with my former business associates? Will Mikayla betray some hidden knowledge?

I watch her, but she's cutting meatballs with her fork and pushing the pieces around on her plate, same as every year. In approximately eleven minutes my father will catch her eye and she, smiling, will push her plate over for him to finish.

The business associates load their greedy plates with seconds. They attack the serving bowl. A gingham sleeved-arm reaches to poach from my plate. I reach for the wine bottle. Empty.

At the door, the thug says to my mom, "Blackie's tired of you people holding out on us." I shoot the former associates what I hope is a withering glance that will drive them from the family home. I hear Mom ask the thug, "Want some dinner?"

No. This table is already overcrowded with the unwelcome. I go to the door.

"Ma," I say. "Are you kidding?"

The thug puts his nicotine hands up like *hey, back off.* "She asked."

My mother gives me her disapproving look. "You've always been ungrateful."

I glare. Her looking back at me like, *what*. In my best tough-guy voice I say to the thug, "You come to my mother's door?" I shape my mouth into offended-plus-angry. "Violate the family table?"

He flushes. Looks at his feet.

"Set up a meet," I say. I like the B-movie- feel and I'm curious what he'll do.

He raises his head, energized, like *finally someone gets it*. "I'll talk to the boss."

Good. Back at the table, Mikayla, arms folded. "Kid," I inquire, "How do you account for this?"

"How should I know?" Whiny undertones. "That guy smells bad." Her meatballs now in front of my father, the rat. "Why won't you believe me?"

It's a fair question. It occurs to me, but I don't say, *because you're my kid*. Unfair. She's a person of reasonable integrity for her developmental stage. But there are issues of judgment. Last year she made a killing in water futures – how she's able to buy her building now. I asked what about the downtrodden, the thirsty? What about the various ethics involved? (Good thing the ex- wasn't there – ethics is a word I'm no longer allowed to say in front of her.) "I'm in fifth grade," the kid said. "We haven't learned ethics yet."

So I have my doubts. "We're family," I say. "What are you hiding?"

The ex- gives me the death glare. *"Really?"*

I make the face like, *I don't know what I'm doing wrong.*

Mom, who doesn't like feeling inhospitable, bangs plates together to clear the table. The kid, tight-lipped. Revealing nothing. The boyfriend, eyes blinky like he's guilty, but that's maybe me projecting how much I don't like him. The former associates I shoot a glance like, *you who are dead to me, stay out of this.* Dad sulks, his birthday lost to intrigue and the threat of small-time violence.

The next afternoon I'm watching out the window, and I don't see anyone lurking who could be the mysterious Blackie Donovan.

It's early shades of dusk when my phone rings. A nicotine smell wafts through the tiny speaker. "When your doorbell rings, answer it."

When I do, the first thing I see is a large fist moving fast until it breaks my nose. Attached to that fist is a linebacker-shaped Black man with kind eyes. I wince and brace for more. "You're not Mikayla's father," he says. He smells of lilacs.

I take a fighting stance and say, through blood and busted cartilage, "Am so."

His fist shocks my face a second time. "Mikayla's Black," he says.

Long-buried questions of paternity pop to the surface. "Wait. She is?" Something doesn't add up here but I'm raw and bleeding on my porch. "What do you mean?"

Again, the fist to the face. "Mikayla is also 25."

I see his point. I would have been eight when she was born. It's possible I've never felt such pain. My face, my whole head a house on fire. I indulge my curiosity. "Blackie, huh?"

His fist launches a fourth time, but stops short of my snout. Mercy and grace. "I was a nine-year-old in an Irish gang." Maybe he senses my empathy. He lowers his guard. "You don't choose your nicknames."

"Don't I know it." We stand there awkwardly, neither of us sure what's next. I watch his face soften. I drip blood on my porch.

He hands me his handkerchief. "We're all defined by others' perceptions."

I'm thinking *amen*, and I'd bet he's suffered that more than I have, but I'm steering this conversation toward safer ground.

"What did she do, your Mikayla?" I ask through wet cloth.

"That's between me and her." Then, softer. "How old's yours?"

"Eleven."

"Great age." We're building a parental solidarity.

I show him a picture. His face clouds. Big, puffy cumulus.

"*What?*" I ask.

I watch Blackie Donovan choose his words like rare fruit. "She ever go by Mikey?"

I don't like this. "Sometimes," I say. Hockey-face calls her that.

Blackie's face clouds darken. His eyes grow big. "Nothing. Never mind." Something timid has crept into his voice. "She's lovely. You tell her I said so. Tell her my man won't be bothering her anymore."

The next night, as we dine on chili rellenos, I'm telling the ex- how the kid's off the hook, and that I've apologized for doubting her. I don't tell her how I may be slow on the uptake but I can still add two and two, or how I spent the morning in my favorite diner talking with Blackie about a possible alliance, and I'm feeling good, keeping a poker face, letting the ex- enjoy my swollen nose and sure as hell not letting her know this particular lemon is already oozing lemonade when the doorbell rings.

I answer, all irritated like *I thought we were done with this*. But when I open the door, what I see is my former associates, eyes hooded, lips pinched, huddled on my porch in black leather jackets that reek of nicotine.

No problem. I pull out my phone, thumb to favorites, and dial the kid.

"Daughter," I say, "I need a favor."

Counting Backwards
by Kevin McLellan

your impatience
for a response

and an unwillingness

to identify one
remains / in other

words if you took

delirium no one would
find you / a poor

historian / alert

like a mockingbird
at nightfall / the

incessant assorted

notes / chatter
the form of waiting

and overexposure

The Rise of Negation
by Kevin McLellan

your memories like cells / these

imperfect combinations continue
dividing and multiplying in the

swelter today / yes / sometimes

unable to manage self-control
you lie or change the topic / basil

and honeysuckle in the kitchen

smell indistinguishable / yet you
can't ignore the yelling just

outside your window / recall

your carefree childhood / must
believe in a soaking russet half

From the Inside Out
by Kevin McLellan

He crossed your horizon

and left / it doesn't get
easier / you carved

the memory of him out

of your chest / let the heart-
shape rest in a green

cardboard container (quart-

sized, the kind for
berrying) on the side

of the road / your body

a mountain pass / a car
drives up the right side

of your lower back / all

the way to your left
shoulder blade / no / this

the trajectory of the scar

from the accident / you
neglected to use a filter

while listening to him

punish you / you took it all
the way to the horizon

Hash Pipe

by Amy Bernstein

*I*n high school, he was cool every day. Not stupid cool, like the ones who were stoned all the time. Stoned often, but not always. Long hair, blond and dirty, tied back in a ponytail. Too thin, jeans belled at the bottoms. Didn't participate in SDS, or theater club, or any of that stuff. I was in the band.

Each day I watched him walk down the hall in his sexy way, sliding to the rock music in his head, or swaying back and forth, pelvis thrust out while strumming an imaginary guitar. He cut classes and slouched off down the street alone. Once I followed him to the ugly little house where he lived with his brother and their grandparents. I stood outside, waiting for a shade to move.

I tried to be like him, sad and aloof as a flying ace. I sat alone in the lunchroom, hoping he would notice. But we only spoke one time. That day he was in the cool section of the cafeteria, eating lunch with a slender beauty; a deer of a girl with brown eyes like mushroom caps. I was sitting as near as I could get in the uncool section, watching him slyly as usual from behind my paper bag. He and she were flawlessly high. They laughed and she shoved him.

Something dropped out of his pocket and hit the floor. It didn't shatter; it just lay there white on the dirty tiles, a hash pipe carved from a seashell.

If one of the cafeteria ladies saw it, she would take it away. Maybe he would be expelled. I waited. Then I stood up. I walked myself over. I picked up the pipe, and held it for a moment; it was smooth as sea glass and warm from his skin.

"Hey," I said, my voice surprisingly strong, "you dropped this."

He turned his head and looked at me for the first time. Up close, his green eyes had dark shadows under them, and his thin lips turned down at the corners. Then he smiled, and the shadows vanished and his eyes incandesced neon. He laughed, a wild high-pitched laugh.

"Man, what a dope I am." He reached out his long-fingered hand. As I slid the shell onto his palm, our fingertips touched for a second and static electricity sparked and burned between us. This made him laugh more and jerk his hand back, but I would have kept mine there until it blistered.

"No, wait, Babe, keep it. I can't take it where I'm going any-way."

"Really?" I wanted to say, Going, going where? Don't go. But I had no right.

He placed the pipe carefully on my hand, touching it again briefly with a soft goodbye stroke of the finger that did not stray onto my palm. Then he turned back to the deer girl.

Babe, I thought, he called me "Babe."

He had gotten a low draft number and, out of sadness I guess, he went. I was in his younger brother's class. The brother was every-thing that he was not: popular, tall, in student government, good at sports, and not cool at all. This younger brother was not old enough for the draft. He came to see me and asked to look at the pipe.

"He gave that to you?"

"Yeah." I nodded slowly, in a cool way, as if it was no big thing.

He started hanging out with my friends and me. He came to my dumb band concerts and sat in front of me while I played. One day he came out afterward to the Dairy Queen with us band kids and sat down beside me.

"Would you go to prom with me?"

"Oh, Man, you must be kidding. Proms are so lame. And, why would I go with you?" His face slumped then, disappointed as a box of love-letters at a yard sale, a look I was going to see on that face for years, waking and sleeping, though I didn't know it then.

"Please, just come with me."

The prom was not cool at all, but anyway, we went. We danced; he was a good dancer, actually. We snuck outside and smoked in the parking lot. He tried to kiss me but was nice when I said no. His brother wouldn't have been so nice about it, I thought. It would have been "put up or shut up" with him. We went out together for three years and he was always nice when I wouldn't make out. I waited for his brother to come home. We graduated. Then, one night, he took me to a fancy restaurant with red velvet curtains, and white tablecloths, he got down on one knee and told me that he loved me.

"I want us to be together forever." Not cool at all. He offered me a shiny gold ring. He placed it on my palm and stroked it with one finger, a soft goodbye. I had his brother's pipe in my pocket that night. I keep it with me still. But in the end, because he had noticed me, because he was kind and still around, and because he stroked that ring goodbye the same as his brother had stroked my pipe, I married him.

We have been married for twenty long years. Now and then, when his face slumps into disappointment or I finger the pipe in my pocket, I wonder if I did wrong by both of us, going with him to the prom and all that followed, when I loved the other one. But without all that, I wouldn't have my youngest son. He has long dirty blond hair, lonely green eyes, and that sad, cool way about him. I love the other children, of course, I do, but not like I love this boy. This one looks and acts just like my husband's older brother; the cool one, still missing in action over there.

Off.

by Lauren Marie Scovel

As usual, you start with the door to the fire escape. You see that the latch is locked but you unlock it anyway. Now pull twice to make sure that the deadbolt is also locked. It is. It always is. Relock the latch and tug two more times. The doorknob is ancient and already wobbles when you grab on to it. You wonder how much longer it will last.

Now back up to face the stove. This is the most important part of your routine, your nighttime ritual. Check that all four burners are off, first by moving your eyes slowly from left to right over the knobs. *Off, off, off, off.* Repeat from right to left. *Off, off, off, off.* Now watch the burners themselves, moving from left to right. *Off, off, off, off.* Then right to left. *Off, off, off, off.*

Now walk slightly to the right and press on the door to the refrigerator to ensure that it is fully closed. It is. It always is. Back up to the entrance of the kitchen. Check that the coffee maker is unplugged. Now move back into the kitchen to look at the stove for a second time. First the knobs: *Off, off, off, off; off, off, off, off.* Then the burners: *Off, off, off, off; off, off, off, off.* See that the latch on the fire escape is locked. It still is. Turn off the kitchen light.

Cross through the living room to the front door and check that the deadbolt is locked. Tug on it once and listen to it knock against the frame of the door. It's locked. Walk towards your room and eye the kitchen again from your doorway. Focus on the stove. *Off, off, off, off; off, off, off, off. Off, off, off, off; off, off, off, off.* Turn off the living room light. Watch the stove for the last time in the darkness (you would see a flame if a burner was on). *Off, off, off, off; off, off, off, off. Off, off, off, off; off, off, off, off.* Turn to the front door and see the deadbolt lock illuminated by light on the other side of the door. It's locked. Exhale and turn to go to sleep.

There are good nights and bad nights. On a good night, the routine stops here. On a bad night, you will have to repeat or add steps. Maybe you remember that the kitchen window was open earlier, and you want to confirm that it is now closed. Maybe you realize that the far-right burner looked different today. If you're drunk or exhausted, you will assume you missed something. If someone comes home after you've retreated, you may have to start over. You may re-emerge from your room almost instantly, or you may wait until you've settled into bed. The routine is cumulative: if you go back to the stove, you must re-check the refrigerator, coffee maker, and the front door. If you return to the fire escape, you must start from the beginning.

On a good day, the routine takes two minutes. On a bad day, it can take up to ten.

You do an abridged version of the routine whenever you leave the apartment. If someone else is home, merely check the stove once. If you are the last one to leave, look at the stove at least twice. When you leave, remember to lock the deadbolt then push on the door three times from the outside to ensure that it latched. Walk halfway down the stairs, then look back to check that the door is closed.

The daytime routine is precautionary, so that you can fully enjoy your plans for the day. The day you reunited with your boyfriend after the summer apart, you checked the stove three times. You didn't want to be thinking about the stove when you saw him for the first time in four months. Once last summer, you were housesitting and left for the evening to see a show with your family. You did four sweeps of the house, and took pictures at each step in case you worried while you were out.

You don't remember exactly when you started doing routines, but you know that the day you don't is the day that something goes wrong. You develop routines the way a dog develops its territory. Your routine in your apartment commenced instantly, but your routine at your boyfriend's house took a few months. The routine at your parents' house is much more elaborate, their stove much more complicated. They have a sliding glass door that occasionally doesn't lock into place.

You spent years convincing yourself that it wasn't OCD because you'd never been afraid of germs. You still don't really know what it is but you know it's obsessive and compulsive. When you read books for class, you will mark passages two or three times before they look right. You bought erasable highlighters so that you could fix lines that weren't perfectly straight. You rewind shows and movies if you miss six words of dialogue. If you can't rewind, you try to find the clip again later. You still wonder what that room looked like on an episode of *House Hunters* you watched recently.

You've spent ten years training to be an actor, so you are good at hiding it. You're a sober drunk and a subtle obsesser. If your roommates are still awake when you do the routine, you will act more casual about it. Worse case, you can get up later to redo it.

When you are alone, it's much more focused and serious. It's more official that way. You wonder if your neighbors can see.

You got a new roommate this year, and she slept on the couch for a week before her furniture was delivered. She woke up in the middle of the night to see you staring over the stove.

"What are you doing?" she asked.

"Just locking up," you said, "This is a thing that I do."

Another roommate knows about your routine and—at your request—does an abridged version if you aren't home for the night (you stress the importance of the stove and the front door). Your boyfriend knows why you leave the room right before bed. You will never be able to come home and go straight to sleep. You know that the day you do is the day that something goes wrong.

It only takes a few minutes, but you wonder if years from now you will add up those minutes and repetitions and *off, off, off, off*s and regret them. You wonder if you will do this when you have your own house or kids. You wonder if it will get progressively better or progressively worse.

Sometimes you blame your family. They allowed you to move so far away for college, and your mother always taught you to double check your work. The day you don't do it is the day that something goes wrong.

You know that there's a problem, and you know that it's ridiculous. You've always been logical. You know that no one's died of not obsessing. You know the day you don't do it is the day that something goes wrong.

Tonight, your boyfriend is going to stay over. You will slip out of bed and do your routine before crawling in next to him again: fire escape, stove, fridge, coffee maker, stove, front door, stove, front door. It will only take two minutes. Five at the most. Maybe ten.

Tomorrow, he will leave at 5:30 in the morning for work. You will lock the deadbolt behind him then check the stove again before going back to sleep: *Off, off, off, off; off, off, off, off.*

Adiabatic Theorem
by Suzanne S. Rancourt

A light bell
the weight
the scent of almonds dangling kite tails
from the spine of a Foehn wind
before the rapid descent of a katabatic
Oroshi voids the gullied rain shadow

A bird invades a larch tree
rapid backstroke of wings replicates
the sound of playing cards
clothes pinned to my bicycle spokes -
Harley rumble -
my green-hand-me-down-Schwinn
strategically placed by you, my sister,
to be run over by Dad's truck
twisted paralyzed and silent
How could I betray you
after you confessed?

After you confessed
that it was you who threw me out of the
truck window at 40 mph
an infant stone, I hit dirt -
rolled along the roadside
the scar on my left frontal arch
now slips into crow's feet
Who knows what pebbles of lies are caught

SUZANNE S. RANCOURT

in the crop of birds caught
by the larch tree caught
by the wind caught
by my ear and the spider that crawls
from hair to hair on my gossamer arm - an
evening glove of magic
the spider - silent to my ears - but my hair
hears her humming
songs of truth while she weaves while
she climbs my alpine shoulder, my meadow
nape of neck

How could I betray you?
After the intimacy of struggle?
The weave of swallowed words?

Paul Laurence Dunbar Reveals How We All Wear the Mask
by Chris Hartman

*"He sang of love when earth was young, /
And love itself was in its laze, /
But ah the world had turned to praise, /
A jingle in a broken tongue."*

— Paul Laurence Dunbar, "The Poet"

For his 2018 documentary *Paul Laurence Dunbar: Beyond the Mask*, Ohio University professor Frederick Lewis spent 8 years researching highlights of the personal life and career of one of the most influential Black poets, Paul Laurence Dunbar (1872-1906). "I was fascinated," Lewis writes, "by the way Dunbar navigated the period after Reconstruction, commonly called the nadir of American race relations, that saw the rise of Jim Crow. A horrific time of lynchings and legal segregation."

Dunbar, the son of former slaves, felt the sting of both discrimination and racial stereotyping throughout his life. He left a complicated artistic legacy. Authors and luminaries in his lifetime and since have hailed his work, but for different reasons. Maya Angelou, who appears in the documentary (her breakthrough memoir *I Know Why the Caged Bird Sings* is titled after one of his lyrics), found in Dunbar a smoldering anger and dignity, an insistence on integrity in a culture that treated him as an 'other'. Dunbar's contemporaries, though, valued most the poetry he wrote in a dialect that seemed to contribute to precisely such 'othering'. Strongly influenced by the plantation idiom and pronunciation featured by white southern writers like Irwin Russell, Thomas Nelson Page, and Joel Chandler Harris, these dialect poems risked reinforcing a jolly and fanciful image of those who had been enslaved. William Dean Howells, in an enthusiastic 1896 review of Dunbar's second poetry collection, *Majors and Minors*, offered a compliment whose sincerity makes it all the more backhanded: like Scottish poet Robert Burns, Howells wrote, Dunbar was "least himself when writing literary English."

The questions of who Dunbar's "self" was, and what literary vision shaped his work, are the subject of *Beyond the Mask*.

Paul Laurence Dunbar was the youngest son of Joshua and Matilda Dunbar, who had been enslaved and who fled Louisville, Kentucky after the Emancipation Proclamation in 1863. Joshua, twenty years Matilda's senior, had crossed the Ohio River from Kentucky, and made his way to Canada via the Underground Railroad. He soon returned to the U.S., where he joined the 55th Massachusetts Infantry Regiment. Matilda, in the meantime, settled in Dayton, where she became a laundress in the homes of white residents.

Dunbar's mother Matilda was devoted to her son's educational advancement, hoping he would decide to become a minister. In fact, even before he was a teenager, Dunbar gave readings at church and afternoon school assemblies where, due to his dignified carriage, he was dubbed "The Deacon." Among his earliest admirers was classmate and later inventor Orville Wright.

Dunbar edited his high school newspaper, the (Dayton) *High School Times*, and contributed to a student magazine, *Tomfoolery*. He also wrote for the *Dayton Tattler* (underwritten by Orville Wright). Though *The Tattler* lasted only three issues, Dunbar managed to expose numerous social and political problems in the city – including the Democratic Party's buying of Black votes.

Graduating from Central High School in June, 1891, Dunbar found his hopes of suitable employment dashed by the color line: he briefly took a job as a janitor at Dayton's National Cash Register Company. He next applied for a clerical position with Dayton attorney Charles W. Dustin, who could only offer him employment as an "elevator boy," for which he would be paid $4 a week for 11-hour days. Even so, Dunbar managed the time to write a western short story, "The Tenderfoot," which he sold to the Kellogg Syndicate of Chicago for $6.

It was during this time that one of Dunbar's most notable orations took place, at the Central Literary Club of the Western Association of Writers' gathering in June, 1892. Dunbar gave the opening address. Dr. James Newton Matthews, a physician and poet, and one of Dunbar's patrons, wrote of Dunbar's performance in a letter to the *Indianapolis Journal* newspaper, praising him (and, in its racialized language, prefiguring some of his struggle for critical acceptance):

> Great was the surprise of the audience to see stepping lightly down the aisle a slender Negro lad, as black as the core of Cheops Pyramid. He ascended the rostrum with the coolness and dignity of a cultured entertainer. He was applauded to the echo between the stanzas, and heartily encored. He then disappeared from the hall as suddenly as he had entered it – none believing it possible that one of his age and color could produce a thing of such evident merit.

Self-publishing his first collection of poetry, *Oak and Ivy*, released just before Christmas, 1892, Dunbar made allusions to the elevator he minded, and that enclosed him. The last stanza of "Sympathy" has become immortal:

I know why the caged bird sings, ah me,
When his wing is bruised and his bosom sore—
When he beats his bars and he would be free;
It is not a carol of joy or glee,
  But a prayer that he sends from his heart's deep core,
But a plea, that upward to Heaven he flings—
I know why the caged bird sings!

Following the success of *Oak and Ivy*, Dunbar was hired by the *Dayton Herald* to write a feature piece on the Dayton Soldiers Home. Dunbar made his emotional return to that place, where his late father had resided for so many years. His next piece for them was to be a feature on the 1893 World's Columbian Exposition in Chicago, a World's Fair on the 400th anniversary of Columbus's voyage to the New World. But Dunbar's pay didn't cover his expenses, so while in Chicago he moonlighted as both a hotel waiter and a lavatory attendant.

At the Fair, Dunbar met Joseph H. Douglass, a classical violinist and the grandson of abolitionist and statesman Frederick Douglass. At the time, Frederick Douglass was serving as Ambassador to Haiti, and was overseeing that country's exhibitions at the Fair. Douglass offered Dunbar a job as his assistant, paying him out of his own pocket.

Together they attended "Colored Americans Day," an alternate event organized by Black leaders in protest at the near-exclusion of the Black experience from the official Exposition. Dunbar read several of his poems at the event. Douglass was moved to remark,

"I regard Paul Dunbar as the most promising young colored man in America."

Owing to his friendship with Douglass, Dunbar's reputation was enhanced both nationally and internationally. But 1893 also saw one of America's worst financial panics; unemployment rates shot up past 35%, and Dunbar's home was threatened with foreclosure. Only a last-minute loan from Toledo attorney Charles Thatcher, who had recently befriended Dunbar, saved him and his mother from eviction. Dunbar learned that the man who had taken his elevator job at the Callahan Building had quit, so he returned to the job.

In the spring of 1895, after nine years of rejection, *Century Magazine* accepted three of Dunbar's poems, including "Negro Love-Song," inspired by Dunbar's brief time as a hotel waiter at the Chicago Fair. Its first stanza:

> Seen my lady home las' night,
> Jump back, honey, jump back.
> Hel' huh han' an' sque'z it tight
> Jump back, honey, jump back.
> Hyeahd huh sigh a little sigh,
> Seen a light gleam f'om huh eye,
> An' a smile go flittin' by —
> Jump back, honey, jump back.

The refrain, "Jump back, honey, jump back," was yelled out by the waiters at anyone blocking the swinging kitchen doors of the hotel dining room as they rushed through, armed with full trays of food.

Reading the Boston-based Black magazine, *The Monthly Review,* Dunbar was struck by one of its writers, a teacher and New Orleans native named Alice Ruth Moore. The fan letter he wrote her contained lightly-veiled amorous references. By this time, Dunbar was heading a Black newspaper, *The Indianapolis World*. He started courting Alice, writing poems to her, and published one of her stories, "The Willow Tree," in *The Indianapolis World*.

Around this period, Dunbar received an invitation to speak at the Toledo State Hospital for the Mentally Insane. Its superintendent, Henry A. Tobey, was a great admirer of Dunbar's poetry. Tobey's facility was atypical in that it didn't treat its patients like inmates in cell blocks, but instead housed them in rows of attractive Victorian-style structures. Dunbar's verse was part of the humane program of "amusements" Tobey provided his patients, and it was the beginning of a lifelong friendship between the two men. Charles Thatcher, who had rescued the Dunbars' home from foreclosure, joined with Tobey to co-finance a second volume of Dunbar's poetry.

In September of 1895, the Cotton States Exposition opened in Atlanta and Tuskegee Institute president, Booker T. Washington, arguably the most prominent Black voice to fill the void left by the recent death of Frederick Douglass, was a headline speaker. Washington advanced an economic separatist theory of society, with Black men pursuing vocational trades such as farming, carpentry, and construction, and the women domestic arts, such as hairdressing. Washington had asserted that no race will prosper until it understands there is as much dignity to be achieved by plowing a field as by writing a poem. This dismayed Dunbar, who wrote in response, "I do not believe the soul of a man, whose soul is turbulent with a message that should be given to the world from the pulpit or press should shut his mouth and shoe horses."

Douglass' passing left Dunbar despondent, and he responded in the best way he knew how – with a laudatory poem, "Frederick Douglass." Its ending stanza makes for a powerful coda to the life of a formidable man:

> Oh, Douglass, thou hast passed beyond the shore,
> But still thy voice is ringing o'er the gale!
> Thou'st taught thy race how high her hopes may soar,
> And bade her seek the heights, nor faint, nor fail.
> She will not fail, she heeds thy stirring cry,
> She knows thy guardian spirit will be nigh,
> And, rising from beneath the chast'ning rod,
> She stretches out her bleeding hands to God!

Later that year, Dunbar's second volume of poems, *Majors and Minors*, was published. It included what is widely regarded as Dunbar's most important and well-known poem, "We Wear the Mask," that begins,

> We wear the mask that grins and lies,
> It hides our cheeks and shades our eyes,—
> This debt we pay to human guile;
> With torn and bleeding hearts we smile,
> And mouth with myriad subtleties.

The poem lends to many interpretations, but has mostly been taken—as Frederick Lewis' documentary takes it—as capturing the smiles worn by Black people as they endure in the face of daily doses of racial injustice perpetrated by white people.

Returning to Toledo, Dunbar spent an evening at a performance of "Shore Acres," a play starring James Hearn, known as "the American Ibsen." Upon hearing this, Tobey sent Dunbar to the Boody House hotel, where Hearn was staying, to drop off a copy of *Majors and Minors*. Hearn was so enamored of the poems, he wrote Dunbar to say he intended to show the book to the eminent novelist William Dean Howells. Consequently, the June 27, 1896, issue of *Harper's Weekly* featured a glowing review of Dunbar by Howells.

CHRIS HARTMAN

Serendipitously, this same issue focused heavily on the 1896 presidential race, so it quickly sold out from newsstands, gaining Dunbar even greater visibility.

The consensus among Dunbar's Toledo-based patrons was that he needed to capitalize on Howells' review. Major James B. Pond and his Lyceum Lecture Circuit – that had represented Mark Twain, Henry Morton Stanley and Winston Churchill (who later referred to Pond as "a vulgar, Yankee impresario") – was contacted to manage Dunbar's public appearances.

After becoming Pond's client, Dunbar traveled to Rhode Island and New York. Patron Charles Thatcher had arranged private readings with Narragansett Pier summer residents, including Mrs. Jefferson Davis, known as the "Mother of the Confederacy." Dunbar visited the home of William Dean Howells on Long Island. Howells recounted his own Ohio upbringing, and then agreed to write the introduction to Dunbar's next book, *Lyrics of Lowly Life*. In it, Howells declared Dunbar "the Bard of the Negro race." The racial stereotypes that had accompanied his earlier paean to Dunbar in *Harper's Weekly* were present but now a bit more nuanced.

Major Pond sent copies of *Lyrics* to London, and with favorable reviews following, urged Dunbar to travel to Britain. The night before he sailed for Europe, February 5, 1897, Dunbar attended a party at the Brooklyn home of social reformer Victoria Earle Matthews, where he met Alice Ruth Moore for the first time. The correspondence between Dunbar and Moore had been growing more intimate. Among the invited guests at the Brooklyn party were Booker T. Washington and W.E.B. Dubois, but Dunbar spent the evening exclusively with Alice Ruth Moore. He proposed to her that night.

Beyond the Mask features interviews with Steven M. Allen, who in 2009 wrote and staged *The Dunbar Operas*. These operas, including *Lyrics of Sunshine and Shadows*, *The Poet*, and *Violets and Other*

| 91

Tales, describe the depth and breadth of the love Dunbar and Moore shared for so many years.

Once in London, Dunbar met the American ambassador John Hay, himself a writer of dialect poetry, having published *Pike County Ballads* as a young man. There were also some speaking engagements, and he had tea with the eminent explorer Henry Morton Stanley. But Dunbar was disturbed by the tone of his reviews; they gave the impression he was looked upon more as a curiosity than a serious writer. And now, with the "reading season" over, Edith Pond, the unscrupulous daughter of Major Pond who was managing Dunbar's tour, abandoned him and left the bill for Dunbar's dingy lodgings unpaid.

Ambassador Hay then introduced Dunbar to composer Samuel Coleridge Taylor, who collaborated with him to set seven of his poems to music, known collectively as *African Romances*. They next teamed up for an opera, *Dream Lovers*. Ambassador Hay arranged for a public performance, in which Dunbar read several of his poems, and Taylor accompanied him with music. Dunbar also negotiated the publication of the English edition of *Lyrics of Lowly Life* through Chapman and Hall, whose authors had included Charles Dickens. But because of money difficulties, Dunbar had to return home. After Edith Pond refused to purchase him a ticket, Dr. Tobey wired him the money.

Now relocated to Washington, Dunbar continued writing a novel he'd begun overseas, *The Uncalled*. With protagonists never specifically identified as black or white, *The Uncalled* was seen as Dunbar's rebuttal to William Dean Howells' assertion that Black authors had to write about Black experiences in certain ways. He also collaborated with Will Marion Cook, who earlier had arranged a musical composition of Dunbar's poem "Negro Love-Song" with the title "Jump Back." The new one-act musical's title was *Clorindy; or The Origin of the Cake Walk*.

CHRIS HARTMAN

In March of 1898, after years of living apart, Dunbar and Alice Moore decided to quietly marry. Alice subsequently resigned her teaching position in New York and moved to be with Dunbar and his mother in Washington. And in July, *Clorindy* became the first performance of an all-Black musical comedy on Broadway. Dunbar attended the opening, but was discouraged that much of his writing had been edited out in favor of more dance numbers.

In the two decades following the failure of Reconstruction, Black Americans lost many of the gains they had made to emerging Jim Crow laws. With Jim Crow came a resurgence of the Ku Klux Klan, and widespread lynching of Black people. In November of 1898, the only Black newspaper in Wilmington, North Carolina was burned to the ground by white supremacists – killing more than a dozen residents. And though 2,000 whites had participated in this tragedy, *Collier's* magazine, in its coverage of the event, illustrated only Black citizens rioting. Dunbar responded in a column that was carried by several newspapers around the country: "For so long, the Black man believed that he is an American citizen. Of that he will not be easily convinced to the contrary. It will take more than the burnings or lynching of North and South."

In 1899, Dunbar's collection of poems, *Lyrics of the Hearthside*, was published, which included one of his most tender poems, "Little Brown Baby." Shortly after its publication, he was diagnosed with tuberculosis and retreated to convalesce in New York's Catskill Mountains. This led to his next book, *Poems of Cabin and Field*, which included eight previously published poems that had originally appeared in volumes with racist illustrations by Edward Kemble. This time Dunbar collaborated with the Camera Club of the Hampton Normal Agricultural and Trade Institute in Virginia, a group seeking to reform images of Black people in popular culture

The Dunbars next traveled west to Denver, Colorado, where Dunbar was welcomed by the local newspapers as "The Poet

| 93

Laureate of the Negro Race." After purchasing a small home near Denver, he began writing essays as well as a new novel. *Love of Landry* was a romantic western tale, but as was becoming a regular refrain, it was panned by reviewers as unconvincing in its portrayal of white characters. He had better fortunes with his story collection, *The Strength of Gideon*, which concentrated largely on stories of the old South, as well as Biblical parables.

Dunbar's writing had never been more popular, but his health was beginning a precipitous decline. This was exacerbated by his physician actually prescribing alcohol to alleviate symptoms, causing Dunbar to drink to excess. And as if that weren't bad enough, he was also prescribed heroin tablets. Unsurprisingly, the Dunbars' marriage was in trouble, as he would display bouts of anger stemming from his illness, constant travel, and the criticism of his writing. One evening in 1902, Dunbar became violent with Alice. She left him and never reconciled, despite his plaintive letters.

Back in New York, Dunbar rejoined collaborator Will Marion Cook, adding lyrics to Cook's musical *In Dahomey*. It would become the first full-length musical comedy written and performed by Black artists to be featured on the mainstage of a Broadway theater.

Dunbar's output at this time was prodigious. His poem *When Malindy Sings* was inspired by his mother Matilda's love of the old Negro spirituals. He also published a fourth novel, *Sport of the Gods*, which abandoned the motif of white Americans for a southern Black family forced to move north when their patriarch is imprisoned. During the Harlem Renaissance, it was adapted into a motion picture of the same name from Reol Pictures, one of the earliest studios that produced films for Black audiences. Dunbar also dedicated a new volume of poetry to "Miss Catherine Impey," who had founded Britain's first anti-racist magazine, *Anti-Caste*, to which he was a contributor.

As the consumption Dunbar suffered from took him closer to death, his wife Alice (they had never divorced) saw the headlines about his condition. She attempted to reach him through his friend and doctor, Bud Burns. But on February 9, 1906, Dunbar succumbed. He was just 33 years old.

Matilda lived at the house in Dayton for the next 28 years, supported by her son's publishing royalties and the kindness of family and friends. There, she greeted admirers of her son, including such luminaries of the Harlem Renaissance as Langston Hughes and Countee Cullen. Alice Moore Dunbar-Nelson (Dunbar's widow remarried following his death), published *The Dunbar Speaker and Entertainer*, and in addition to her career as a teacher, writer, and activist, she lectured widely on Dunbar's literary accomplishments for the next thirty years.

According to Frederick Lewis (whose other documentaries include a film about the artist and explorer Rockwell Kent), "What I really wanted to develop very carefully [in *Beyond the Mask*] was the structure of the documentary – weaving contemporary segments about Dunbar's legacy in with the archival materials that provide historical context and tell his biography." He also was pleased that nearly thirty of his students at Ohio University shot footage for the film in Chicago, Washington, D.C., New Orleans, and elsewhere, in addition to editing and conducting research.

Paul Laurence Dunbar has been memorialized in numerous biographies, in opera, and a hip hop song, Canton, Ohio-based rapper Jeán P.'s homage, "We Wear the Mask." He is the subject of paintings and sculptures. Dunbar's name adorns numerous elementary and high schools around the country and he shares the name of an historic district in Dayton, Ohio with the famous aviators, Orville and Wilbur Wright.

Dunbar himself was deeply conflicted about his writing and its reception, often expressing frustration at white literary lights like William Dean Howells, who even as they praised his representations of Black vernacular, essentially ignored the cultural significance of his standard English verse and his experiments with European and Western American regionalisms.

    A life of contradiction, profound insecurities, poor health, and the often dismissive and condescending attitudes of fellow authors and the reading public, tempered Dunbar's literary accomplishments. Even so, his poetry and prose have moved and inspired generations of students of all races and cultures. According to the Black poet, novelist, and civil rights activist James Weldon Johnson, "[Dunbar] was the first to rise to a height from which he could take a perspective view of his own race. He was the first to see objectively its humor, its superstitions, its short-comings; the first to feel sympathetically its heart-wounds, its yearnings, its aspirations, and to voice them all in a purely literary form."

    Though at times Frederick Lewis' *Paul Lawrence Dunbar: Beyond the Mask* moves with a pace revealing an editing style that is insistent about including the work of too many hands, it succeeds in providing powerful assurance that Dunbar will maintain his place as a an enduring historical and literary figure in America – and one particularly relevant and necessary in these uncertain times.

Moose

by Deborah Mead

It's Emilie who spots it first, a baby turtle, motionless at the end of the cul-de-sac. She almost misses it entirely, dusted as it is with the dry dirt of the pavement. The size of a quarter, the hatchling lies low to the ground, an insignificant disk lost among the grit of the road. A few dull yellow stripes run down the sides of its neck.

Emilie and Rachel squat around it, Emilie poking it gingerly with a stick. The turtle doesn't respond.

"Do you think it's alive?" Emilie asks, tugging her denim skirt more snugly around her knees. She hopes her underwear doesn't show.

"No," Rachel says. "It's dead and it's gross."

"Where'd it come from?"

"Probably the pond over there." Rachel gestures vaguely down the street toward the houses opposite her own. "Must've walked through the backyards."

Emilie tucks a blond strand behind one ear as she gazes down the street at the split-level houses with sagging fences and dandelion-dotted lawns. It's a different neighborhood from hers, and although she has been here many times, it still doesn't feel familiar.

Playdates at her own house are always indoors, in the bright yellow playroom with board games and puzzles stacked quietly on the shelves. But at Rachel's, the girls stay outdoors in the cul-de-sac, playing games with no rules, at least none that Emilie can discern. It's always a little daunting to Emilie, the swath of unstructured and unsupervised time, but she doesn't complain. It's Rachel's house and Rachel's rules, according to the generally accepted code of playdates.

Emilie pokes the turtle again with the stick. It retracts its head.

"Hey, he *is* alive. Look how dusty he is. He must be thirsty."

"Turtles don't get thirsty," Rachel says. "They carry water in their shells. Like little camels."

"I don't think that's true," Emilie says, although she doesn't know for sure. Rachel does sound very confident and Emilie doesn't like to contradict her.

Rachel shrugs and crosses to the edge of the street, where the old stone retaining wall begins. She likes to walk, balance beam-style, across the top of the stones, starting at one low end, gradually climbing higher, until she reaches the highest point of the wall, taller than Emilie's head. At that point, she'll jump back to the pavement and grade herself on how well she sticks the landing. She never scores lower than a 9.5.

Emilie has seen this routine before and isn't watching. "We should name him. What about Shelley? That would be funny."

Rachel wrinkles her nose. "That's dumb. His name's Moose."

Emilie tries out the name in her head. *Moose*. She has to admit it's a good name, better than hers. Getting down on all fours, she lowers one cheek to the pavement. "Hi Moose!"

She sits back up to look at Rachel, now halfway up the wall. "Maybe we should take him back over to the pond."

Rachel shakes her head. "I can't. I'm not allowed to go off the street."

"My mom and I could bring him back when she comes to pick me up."

"Better not. If you drive him back in a car, it won't be the way he came and he'll lose his sense of direction. Then he'll be screwed up for the rest of his life."

Emilie considers this for a minute.

"Well, he's already lost, so it can't make it any worse."

"Yes, it could. He could get more lost." Rachel reaches the top of the wall, an area of tangled brush and thorny vines that leave fine scratches on Rachel's arms and calves. Rachel never seems to mind. Jumping off the wall, she lands feet together with only the slightest wobble when her sneakers skid on the sandy pavement. She thrusts both arms in the air and arches her chest. "9.8!"

"You can't get more lost. You're either lost or you're not lost."

"You can so be more lost. Like if you got lost in a store. You're looking at shoes and then all of a sudden you can't find your dad. If you stay with the shoes, at least you're only a little lost and your dad will probably find you again. But if you go out in the mall, you're a lot lost and you'll probably get kidnapped."

"I guess." Emilie adjusts the Velcro straps on her sandals. "But we'd be bringing him back to where he should be, so we're not making him more lost. We're making him less lost. Or not lost," she adds quietly. She can feel her heart thumping and her face getting warm. She doesn't risk looking at Rachel.

"You're so stupid. You don't know where in the pond he came from. You could put him on the wrong side and then his mother would be looking for him and he wouldn't be where he's supposed to be. She's probably following his scent right now to find him. You better just leave him where he is."

Emilie tries to imagine a much larger version of Moose creeping through the backyards, sniffing in the grass. Did turtles actually do that? Jake the Snake Man had visited their school at the beginning of the year. He'd shown them lizards and snakes and turtles. She can remember him holding up a large turtle, its shell broad as a dinner plate, its stiff feet paddling in the air. She tries to remember what he said about turtles, whether they stayed with their mothers or whether they were on their own after they hatched. She tries to remember but all she can recall is the sight of the pinwheeling feet and her own vague feeling of nausea and pity at being held helpless in the sky.

Rachel turns to face the opposite direction and begins what she calls her "tumbling pass"—three cartwheels followed by a round-off. Emilie watches her. Rachel keeps her legs perfectly straight and spins so effortlessly. Emilie can't do cartwheels. She tries them sometimes on the playground and Rachel grades them, giving her low scores of 3s and 4s. Rachel always says, "You're too slow. You have to push off with your arms more." She always ends up demonstrating a series of perfectly executed cartwheels and round-offs, feet whipping through the air, while Emilie watches. Most of their school recesses involve Emilie watching Rachel. Emilie doesn't mind, though. She's secretly surprised and proud that Rachel even wants to be her friend. She feels sorry that she can't keep up.

Since moving to Warrenford the previous summer, Emilie has found it hard to make friends. At first it wasn't bad—the teacher introduced her as the new girl and asked her questions about her old school, about packing and unpacking, about getting used to a new town. Emilie both squirmed and reveled in the unfamiliar spotlight. At recess and lunch, the other kids asked her more questions—what kind of pets she had (none), whether she could ride a horse (no), how many times she'd been to Disneyland (twice!).

While the other kids were clamoring to get to know the new kid, Rachel hung back, eyeing her warily. Rachel had a wilder look than the other girls, her jeans soiled at the knees, her reddish brown hair cut short, the tight coarse curls sticking stiffly out from her head. Emilie felt Rachel watching her while she sharpened her pencil or checked out her books in the media center. Whenever she looked at Rachel, it seemed that Rachel's dark eyes were already on her.

By the end of the first week of school, the excitement of having a new kid in class had faded. The girls who had wanted to sit next to her now drifted back to the friends they'd had before and Emilie found herself alone. It was then that Rachel made her move.

"Let's cartwheel," she'd abruptly said, and strode off to the far corner of the dusty playground without checking to see if Emilie was following her. Emilie was, of course. In the months to come, there was never any question of what they were going to do on the playground. They were going to do whatever Rachel wanted to do.

Emilie knows her parents worry about her. She hears them at night, her mother's voice quavering, her father's tensely reassuring. She knows what they say. That she has few friends. That Rachel isn't a good influence. That she's too passive, she needs to participate more in school. At her ballet class, Emilie takes her time fixing her hair and adjusting her leotard in the dressing room mirror. She pretends to notice a stray hair or frayed seam, delaying the time when she will have to turn away from the mirror and find something to do with herself, some way to look like she's not helplessly alone. She sneaks peeks at the other girls, jostling one another and laughing. The girls don't exclude her. They don't include her. She is nothing to them.

Her mother encourages her to talk to the other girls, but she doesn't know what to say. Emilie tries asking the girls if they know the steps yet. They do. The conversation ends.

Her mother loses patience with her. "You can't wait for people to seek you out, for things to happen to you. You have to make things happen for yourself. You gotta have a little gumption!"

Emilie doesn't know what gumption is, but she likes the sound of it. She repeats it softly to herself at night and the word feels big and round in her mouth, like chewing five sticks of gum at once.

Now she watches Rachel's quick cartwheels across the cul-de-sac—one, two, three, and the final emphatic round-off. She's seen it so many times by now, dozens of times a day, every day since she's known her. Sometimes Rachel cartwheels through Emilie's dreams.

The street is covered with tiny pebbles, white and beige, many with sharp edges. As Rachel's hands hit the pavement, Emilie winces inside, imagining each sharp stone pressing its edge into soft flesh, leaving little red dents all over her palms. Watching her, Emilie wants to brush off her own hands, massage the palms tenderly. She doesn't know how Rachel can keep going, impervious to the stones.

Moose is still lying in the same spot by the stone wall. He doesn't look good. At least Emilie doesn't think so. He looks tired and dry. She reaches out one finger and touches his shell. Gathering a little more courage, she picks him up with one hand, forefinger and thumb pinching his sides. The shell is surprisingly pliant, giving under the pressure of her fingers like the soft plastic limbs of her Polly Pocket dolls back home. The springy vulnerability fills her with pity and she eases her grip around him. He weighs so little, is so insubstantial, she has to concentrate on not dropping him.

As she raises him toward her face, she's startled to see his bright orange underside. She hadn't expected such a flash of color from his drab exterior. She's about to show Rachel but thinks better of it. Let it be their own secret.

Instead she gently rocks him side to side to see if she can hear any sloshing sound. There is none.

"I don't think there's water in there," she calls to Rachel. Rachel lands her round-off with a flourish and walks over, brushing her hands off on her jeans.

"You know, you shouldn't touch him. The moms won't take care of the babies if they smell like humans. It could be a snapping turtle, too. They can take your finger right off." Rachel snaps her teeth together a few times to demonstrate, making hard clicking sounds.

"He wouldn't do that. He's nice," Emilie says, but she puts the turtle back down. The thing about a mother animal rejecting her baby sounds familiar. She hadn't thought of that.

Studying Moose, Emilie can hear Rachel's cartwheels begin again, each foot grinding the pebbles as it lands. One, two—Emilie is only vaguely aware of counting them off in her head. Suddenly Rachel's hands land on the pavement in front of her, one on each side of Moose. A shadow passes overhead as Rachel's legs arc through the air and land grittily on the street beyond.

"Hey, be careful!" Emilie yells. She bends forward and puts her face down close to Moose's. Moose withdraws his head into his shell. "You scared him," she says softly.

"I'm not scaring him," Rachel laughs. "Your big fat face is what's scaring him. Come on. I'm sick of the turtle. Let's go back. I think my dad picked up a giant bag of Pirate Booty at Costco last night." Pirate Booty is Emilie's big weakness.

Emilie doesn't answer. She is murmuring encouraging words to Moose, who hasn't re-emerged from his shell.

Rachel sighs loudly. "You know he can't understand you, right?"

Emilie sits up and spins to look at Rachel. "Do you have lettuce?"

"I don't know, but we have Pirate Booty."

"He can't eat Pirate Booty."

Rachel rolls her eyes. "Turtles don't eat lettuce either, dummy. Where would they get lettuce in a pond?"

"Come on—let's go see what's in your fridge." Emilie picks Moose up and places him on her palm, carrying him down the street to Rachel's house. She can wash him off later to get rid of her scent, although she's pretty sure his mom isn't coming to get him.

Rachel catches up with her at the bottom of the concrete stoop. "You can't bring him inside. My nana won't like it."

Emilie scans the front yard for shade, finally placing Moose on the sidewalk by a low spindly hedge. She runs back up the steps to the house, brushing past Rachel.

It always takes Emilie's eyes a minute to adjust to the house's dark interior. Only a sliver of daylight penetrates the gap between the heavy plaid curtains. A thin blue haze hovers in the center of the room and Emilie recoils at the smell of stale smoke and ashes. From the television come the solemn sounds of a daytime soap, voices heavy with the mysterious perils of adulthood.

The screen door bangs shut as Rachel comes in behind her. On the sofa, Rachel's grandmother startles at the sound and clutches at the striped afghan, her hands thickly veined and swollen at the knuckles. Raising her head, she glances at the girls, her pale blue eyes red-rimmed and watery. She mumbles something and goes back to sleep.

Emilie has never met Rachel's dad, isn't even sure she has a mother. The only adult she ever sees at Rachel's house is the grandmother, always silent, always peering at her from the couch. Emilie hurries past the living room and into the kitchen.

104 |

She already has the refrigerator door open when Rachel elbows her aside and yanks open the vegetable crisper. "Told you. No lettuce."

Emilie peers over Rachel's shoulder at the shriveled bell pepper, the strawberries coated with white fuzz. "How about the carrots?"

"He doesn't have any teeth—how's he going to eat a carrot?"

"What's this?" Emilie reaches over Rachel to pull out a cellophane package filled with dark limp leaves.

Rachel snatches the bag out of Emilie's hand. "It's spinach. It's gross."

"It's green, though. He might like it. Let's bring him some water, too." Emilie opens the cabinets and drawers, searching through soup bowls and Tupperware containers. Everything is too large for Moose.

Rachel stands to one side, stone silent, as Emilie rummages through her kitchen. Emilie can feel Rachel watching. She knows she better not look back.

Emilie opens the refrigerator again and takes out the grape jelly jar. She unscrews the cap and washes it, running her finger inside the lip to dislodge the old sticky jelly. Filling it with cool tap water, she heads out of the kitchen, telling Rachel to bring the spinach.

Emilie tiptoes past the living room, careful not to wake Rachel's grandmother again. She descends the front steps slowly, trying not to spill water over the rim of the lid. She silently berates herself as drops fall to the ground, leaving dark splotches on the concrete. Rachel isn't behind her.

Emilie kneels next to Moose, but he makes no move to the water. She tilts the lid to pool the water to one side, finally picking him up and dipping his head into the lid. He retreats into his shell. She frowns.

The screen door bangs again and Rachel comes slowly down the steps. She isn't carrying the spinach. She stands only a few feet from Emilie, looming above her, and crosses her arms over her chest.

"My nana says we can't have the spinach. She says you have to leave the turtle alone. It has germs."

Emilie squints up at Rachel. The sun is almost exactly behind her head, backlighting each brown frizzy curl. It makes her head look enormous, her face dark and inscrutable.

Emilie looks away. "He's a brand new baby. He can't have gotten germs yet."

Rachel takes a step closer. "You're at my house. You have to do what my nana says."

Emilie feels a small lump of anger rising in her, but those are the rules of playdates. She knows this. And her mother wouldn't like it if she found out Emilie disobeyed. She sets Moose down on the ground, then pulls her back long and straight like she learned in ballet class.

"When my mom comes I'm going to ask if we can bring Moose home. We have an old goldfish bowl in the garage. He'll like it in there. I can bring him to school tomorrow for circle time. And everybody can play with him at recess."

Rachel smirks. "Your mom isn't going to let you keep him."

"She might. She said we could maybe get a pet when we moved here."

"Parents always say stuff like that when they feel guilty. Your mom's never going to say yes to a turtle. My dad will, though. We had a snake a couple of years ago, so he won't care. I'm going to ask him when he gets home."

"You can't—I saw him first. He's mine!"

106 |

"He came from my street. That makes him mine. Besides, you don't even know how to take care of a turtle. You were going to feed him carrots."

"You were going to feed him Pirate Booty!"

"Was not."

"You haven't even touched him. You're too scared he'll bite your finger off!"

"No, I'm not. I was just trying to get you to stop bothering him. See?" Rachel plucks Moose off the ground and brings him close to her face, crossing her eyes and making loud bovine sounds. "Moooose! Mooooooooose!"

"Be careful with him! He's soft!"

Rachel turns her back on Emilie and deposits Moose onto the end of the driveway, clearing the sidewalk for another victorious tumbling pass. "I'm definitely bringing him into school tomorrow," Rachel says, striding down the sidewalk to her starting point. "You're right. Everyone will love him."

Emilie is blinking back tears. She knows Rachel is right. Her mother will say no. Rachel's father will say yes. And Rachel will bring Moose in to school tomorrow. She can picture it so clearly. Rachel smiling triumphantly in the center of the morning circle, taking credit for spotting Moose at the end of the cul-de-sac, dirty and hungry and close to dead. How she nursed him back to health and saved his life. She can see the kids clamoring around Rachel, begging for a chance to hold Moose, *her* Moose, while Emilie is left on the periphery.

Rachel's feet are slicing through the air, a careening force headed in her direction. After so many cartwheels, so many round-offs, Emilie has fully absorbed the geometry, the physics, of Rachel. She knows how many cartwheels come before the round-off. She knows the distance between Rachel's hands and feet. Knows how fast those feet whip around and exactly where those feet will land.

Darting forward, Emilie grabs Moose and places him back on the sidewalk, directly in Rachel's path. She sits back on her heels and rubs away her tears. She should be trembling, but there is no dread, only certainty about the outcome. She can see it already: the shell crushed flat, cracked into small pieces. Moose's head ground sideways into the pavement, tiny features erased under a smear of skin, blood, gravel. One rear leg, spared the weight of Rachel's sole, pushing weakly at the ground. The image churns her stomach, but she swallows the bile down.

This must be the gumption her mother talked about. The strange surge of will, foreign but hers all the same. It's unsettling to think of it inside her, pitiless and unpredictable.

Rachel finishes her last cartwheel and launches into the round-off. The V of Rachel's legs vanishes with the final snap of her sneakers coming together. Her hands push off from the pavement, her body unleashed and unfolding in the air.

Emilie stands and steps back from Moose, waits to hear Rachel's score.

I Likened Her Hair to a River

by Myron Michael

I never thought I would go through with a one-night stand. Not because I'm religious; although I did die with salvation on the cross that day I stole something for the last time, and since then have had the sword of Damocles hanging over my genitalia. Sex is like a shot of cognac or a glass of wine after a long day of work—and even though I shoot the risk of producing an unplanned life like destroying a once healthy liver—I always, after work, want a shot; to relax, to sleep afterwards and rejuvenate from the lack of sleep that unsettled. I lay a day's worth of wages on the table and go through with it, and it was just as good as collard greens, in some parts, sukuma, at the restaurant; just as good as the snifter of cognac afterwards. So good, I wanted to clip one of the beads from her waist and save it; just in case she, at the end of dinner or at the bottom of the bottle, decided not to see me again. Which she did; she said there are seasons, then went and chopped off her hair, all of it. I went to work and acted as if nothing had occurred, as if it was all a dream, except it takes weeks for me to recycle. Withstanding is why I will never go through with one again, I will never eat that food at that restaurant again, and the last time I had a glass of cognac or wine, the genethliac of my calendar year was approaching with a full Sagittarius moon that I will never celebrate again. Rather, that's how it began, first birthdays went unacknowledged, and then holidays. I even leapt leap year when it came around. Eventually we ran into each other at a produce market, we each had our hand on a crown of broccoli. Being an honest man, I expressed to her what I desired; it had been awhile. She touched her sheared hair and praised how well I looked, but said something about not sleeping with the same man twice, not sleeping with men at all.

Dear Life

by Marisa P. Clark

In the red dirt of the front walk
a whiptail claws a cave
for shelter from the sun.
Inside, she faces out; her wide
mouth shapes a smile. Yes, I
anthropomorphize. What of it?
In the planter a clay statue
of Saint Francis stands amid
snapdragons. A crust of bird shit
streaks between his shoulders.
How fitting. Once, a pigeon shit
on my father's bald head. He winced
and wiped. *It's good luck*, he said,
to be shit on by a bird. In two years
he would be dead. In the hummingbird
feeder, an island of ants floats in sugar
water, site of their gluttonous sweet
death. This morning brought word
of a famous man's suicide, and
I sought escape outside.

Last night I sat on this same porch
as twilight crossed the sky. At 8:45
the barn swallow returned to roost
for the fourth night in a row, one
minute later than the night before
and time enough for me to grow

anxious with waiting. I said hello
and called her sweetheart. She puffed
and huddled on the narrow ledge
beneath the eaves. I wondered why
she had no mate. Too young or old?
Unlucky? Content to spend her nights
alone? These and other questions have
no answer. But evening will find me
here again, seeking her companionship
and reprieve. And when she tucks
her head into her wing, I'll give thanks
for her dear life and mine—for all of life,
worth holding on for. In our shared
darkness, the first stars flicker, faint.

Pastries in the Backcountry

by Tanushree Baidya

I was in the Grand Teton National Park, carrying bear spray, a bell, and a set of instructions memorized in case I ran into a bear. The water-logged trail to Taggart Lake ambled along through a deeply wooded pine forest. The ground was soft, carpeted with fallen wet leaves venting a crimson hue. My boots were soaked. The trees creaked like old wooden doors and the swish of wind in the forest felt like someone shuffling behind a bush ready to pounce. I yelled in a sing song voice "Hey, bear… hey, bear" every 40 seconds or so and wondered (for the umpteenth time that week) whether drawing attention to the fact that I was a lone hiker was a good idea. But the bear safety guidelines had clearly stated: Make noise.

It was the middle of October. The weather had been turning for a couple of days getting colder and unpredictable. There were few tourists in the town and fewer on the trails. The distant haunting cry of an elk followed me to the end of the trail where the storm clouds kept the looming Teton peaks hidden. I stood in awe taking in the view. The greenish crystal-clear glacial lake was nestled high and deep in the valley reflecting the sublime colors of Fall around.

It was a little after two pm. I ate my sandwich by the water, fished out my book, Bruce Chatwin's *In Patagonia*, from my backpack (the other book I was carrying was Bill Bryson's *A Walk in the Woods*) and read for a while. I was distracted and the words I read barely lingered. I contemplated the dark sky above the hidden Tetons. I tried to imagine a clear day, the blue of the sky on the green lake, the image of the peaks on the still water and me splashing about. The lake lit up, interrupting my thoughts, as lightning flashed across the sky. I got up, packed my stuff into the bag, stretched my legs, and instead of continuing on the looped trail, I decided to head back the path I came from.

It was a seventy-five-minute drive, one-way, over the Teton Pass from Grand Teton to my Airbnb in Victor, Idaho. Why Victor, a small town with one stoplight? Reason: it was cheaper than Jackson Hole, Wyoming. I had already spent the first five days of my vacation living and hiking in Yellowstone, which was pricey. So, for the Grand Teton leg of my journey I decided to live outside the park. The fatigue of driving and hiking alone in bear country was getting to me; I had never done a solo trip like this before and I was a new driver in a foreign land.

I had traveled to other parts of America, mostly cities like San Francisco, Miami, Washington, D.C., and New York, but always with a group. After graduate school, then a new job as a data analyst and building a life in a whole new country and culture, traveling solo felt like the next rite of passage, the sign that I had arrived. That I could make it here on my own. Well, that was the speech I gave myself. You see, the trip was initially planned with my father who lived in India. It was going to be his first time in America, first time exploring a foreign land with his daughter. In his youth he had once travelled to Europe but that was for work. Unfortunately, his US tourist visa application got held up for administrative processing (neither my father nor I completely understood why or knew for how long) and I could not find anyone else to travel with on short notice. I struggled with the decision. I could put it off and lose money on the non-refundable flights and reservations, or I could go for it. I was twenty-eight, practically an adult woman here I reminded myself and decided, why the eff not!

On my way back from the park, I stopped for coffee and my fourth croissant of the day —ham and cheese this time—at Jackson Hole. Outside of the unfrequented backcountry trails that I chose to hike, a coffee shop was my second refuge, my safe space, on this trip. The café sat right by the town square, overlooking a little park that had Elk antler bone white arches guarding each entrance. Savoring the coffee, I watched the storm clouds get darker. If my father was here he would have pointed to the dark sky and remarked, "Apt, so very apt for rum and contemplation…" and probably asked me to explain (again) the difference between a cappuccino, a cortado, and a latte. The thought made me smile.

I bought another croissant for the night and left the café. I walked across the park, past a young couple snapping selfies by the arches, a little girl screaming behind a fat squirrel, and got into my car. By the time I crossed the Teton Pass to get to Victor, a snowstorm was raging. Next morning the pass was closed. I was stuck in Victor.

What the hell do I do in backcountry Idaho?

Back in my Airbnb room, I drifted off, lucid dreaming about being on a stage and struggling to say the word Idaho properly in front of a group of people booing (who looked like characters from the show Letterkenny): ee-Dah-ho?

The 2016 presidential election was less than a month away. At the time, I hadn't lived long enough in America to really understand its politics. But, halfway through 2016 especially after the primaries it was hard not to pay attention or not to care. As an immigrant woman of color, and on my own here, there is always some uncertainty that I have to live with. The election rhetoric around immigration and immigrants made me a lot more self-conscious of my status and my place in this country which contributed to a general feeling of unease.

The constant politicization and dehumanization of my mere existence turned my gaze to make sense of the 'New World' that I wanted to call home. I felt the need to categorize the people who seemed to be the dominant voice in categorizing and othering me. It was a slow grinding turmoil seeping into every aspect of my life including interacting with white people, especially on this trip. My liberal Boston friends cautioned me about traveling through places that they called the "red" states. Even though Boston wasn't always actually that liberal, still, their comments got into my head. All week, while driving through Montana, Wyoming, and now Idaho (these states would majority vote for Trump in a month), I'd been inadvertently cautious while interacting with white people; wondering about who they supported because that would apparently tell me all I needed to know about a person.

The next morning, I watched the storm clouds swirling around the back of the snow capped Tetons. It felt drastic, after a rigid itinerary of trails to hike and views to see to suddenly have no plans. My host was up early too and offered me coffee. I asked her what I could do in Victor. She mentioned a thrift store, a library, and for breakfast recommended a European-style bakery café called Pendl's in Driggs, the next town over. "There's not much to do here," she added in monotone. For most of my stay she remained polite and aloof but generous with her coffee. I decided to get breakfast at the café she recommended.

In Victor, it was overcast with a light dusting of snow everywhere. The sky over Driggs, a fifteen-minute drive away, was clear and bright, no sign of the storm. Maybe it was the time of the day and it being off season but downtown Driggs, to me, felt forlorn. I drove through the pallid main street past the post office, a church, the library and some boarded up stores and turned onto a side street. The café, sporting red walls and a sloping green roof shed, stood behind a giant warehouse, trucks and RVs parked all around it. Surprisingly quaint. I entered and like a woman on a mission headed straight to the counter. I ordered an apple strudel with whipped cream, a cinnamon schecknen, a sausage butternut squash quiche, and a steaming cup of Earl Grey to stay. While waiting for my order, I texted a friend in Boston: *I am pretty sure I am the only brown person in this town for miles and miles.* Later I learnt that Driggs per the 2010 census had a population of about 2000, and the racial makeup was ~73% white, and ~31% Hispanic or Latino. I turned to look around the tiny café: all four tables were occupied. The racial diversity in the café was 100% white. I turned back and said, "Oh, maybe. I. Should. Get. All. This. To. Go…" I spoke slowly and deliberately to make sure the young woman at the counter, who had just served me, understood my accent. "Looks pretty full here."

She smiled, adjusting her blue beanie over her blonde bangs, "Sure. Or, maybe if you are friendly enough, or the people here are friendly enough…" her voice trailed off. I stared at her, unsure of what to do next. She smiled even more in a way that felt patronizing, unnerving me further, and said, "The people here are friendly. Let me help you carry your food."

"Oh, that's ok. I can just eat in my car. I have a long drive," I blurted. But by then she had vanished to the back of the café.

I stood there with my pastries. My first two years in America had given way to a strange conditioning. The mere idea of being visible in an unfamiliar place unnerved me. To be that person of color in the room drawing attention. I looked out the café window and stared into the front of a RV parked right outside. There was a man in a red baseball hat with a coffee mug staring right back.

Suddenly the blue beanie lady was by my side guiding me to the nearest table while carrying half my food. "Lannie, can this young woman share your table?" she asked an elderly lady, who was reading the paper.

Lannie was in jeans and a gray hoodie, wearing purple eye shadow, her blonde hair in a short crop. She looked up with a frown and then smiled broadly. The lines on her forehead like crescent marks. "Oh yes, of course!"

"Thank you," I said. Lannie smiled again and moved her cup and plate to make room for mine; she got back to reading her paper occasionally looking my way. I took my jacket off and settled in my seat and, in spite of myself, was glad to get a spot. It was a charming café and I wanted to enjoy my pastries and tea and write in my Moleskin journal about the last days hiking the various titty trails (Teton apparently means nipple in French). I was inspired by *In Patagonia*, its prose evoked a fantastical sense of being that I hoped to emulate in my writing. But first: pastries.

I bit into the strudel, tasting the cinnamon and nutmeg. The filling was a little tart despite the raisins, the dough fluffy and light. "Wow, this is really, really good strudel," I heard myself say around a mouthful. Lannie laughed.

"Yes, they do it well here. Less sweet, too. I like it that way." She sipped her coffee and bit into her scone, watching me.

"So, where are you from?" she asked.

"Boston," I said.

"Oh, is that so?"

I quickly clarified, "Originally, I am from India. I moved to America only two years ago."

"Oh! Only two years? I would have never guessed it. Your English is so good."

"Oh, yeah?" I said without missing a beat. "So is yours."

If my response caused some tension, Lannie did a great job of covering it up with her smile. I knew it was unintentional, not meant to offend, but I was tired of that staid and unnecessary comment (a presumed compliment), like an animal pissing to mark some territory. I took another bite of my strudel and tried to relax a bit.

"Do you come here often?" I asked, taking on a conciliatory tone.

"Oh, yes! It's the only decent bakery in Teton village. Even better than the ones in Jackson Hole. I lived there once, you know," she said. "Traveling alone?"

I told her about my father and his visa issues. Lannie's countenance changed a bit, as if she wasn't quite sure what to ask next.

"Back home, hiking was our thing. We would go to all these places up in the mountains and plains. Feels weird without him," I explained.

"I see. So, you never intended on traveling alone?" she asked. I nodded without saying anything.

"You know," Lannie said. "I never intended on being alone, but here I am."

Her last comment, of course, resonated. The past week, I had spent most of my time hiking alone, avoiding tourist spots and conversation. After the first night of my trip, where I got overwhelmed making conversation with some "friendly" guys from Texas, I avoided sitting at the bar. Most of my interactions had been brief and transient. Now, here I was sharing a table for the first time in a week and, suddenly, I was hungry for a connection. I spoke about the trails I hiked, and the gigantic fireplace and comfy chairs at the Old Faithful Inn in Yellowstone where you can be invisible in a room full of tourists. She told me it'd been a while since she'd made it back there.

We fell silent for a while. I wanted to ask Lannie about her life, get a sense of her politics, what was she doing on a Tuesday morning in a café in a town called Driggs. Why was she alone? But my tongue felt like lead. Questions like, "What do you do?" and "Tell me about your life?" sounded so inane and intrusive. Lannie's voice cut into my thoughts. "They also do the raspberry Danish and the chocolate croissant really well. That's what I am going to get to go." She leaned in and continued, "Once you go farther out, it's really hard to find a good pastry." She put away her newspaper. "Are you?

"Am I what?"

"Are you planning to go farther out?"

"I don't know. Should I?"

"If you're here, might as well."

"Where should I go?" She smiled and proceeded to tell me about Targhee National Forest.

Lannie got ready to leave, saying she was off to a thrift store to buy blue jeans, waist 27, for her niece. "You seem like a waist 27," she added.

"I won't be after all these pastries." At that, she rolled her eyes. Right.

I watched Lannie leave and glanced around the café. Everyone seemed to know each other but no one, except blue beanie lady, had acknowledged Lannie the entire time I was there. I looked out the window and saw Lannie enthusiastically waving my way and pointing at the direction of the thrift store. I smiled and mouthed thank you. I ordered a sandwich for the road and complimented the apple strudel. Blue beanie lady seemed pleased. In the car, I put in the destination on my phone that Lannie had provided then drove for a long time past unending farm lands, hay bales, and granaries, blasting country music on the radio, chuckling at the lyrics. The landscape was completely different. Who'd guess that there was a storm raging just forty-five miles away on snow-capped peaks and dense forest? I had never seen hay bales stacked so tall or driven through landscape so flat and golden. Farmland upon farmland for miles and miles sans people. I was enamored. I kept driving. Finally, a mountain range sprung high up at a distance.

Targhee National Forest was a lesser-known part of Yellowstone and Grand Teton that no tourist really ventured to. None of the guidebooks and websites had mentioned it. But Lannie had said that's where her niece went hiking (and painting; her niece was an artist) and had gushed about the Mesa Falls.

The Upper Mesa Falls, cascading and taking up the entire width of the Snake River before gushing down more than 100 feet into an ancient canyon, was big and powerful. The information board outside the visitor center (closed for the season) had read: *Born of Fire, Shaped by Water*. The Snake river has been slowing, chipping, and chiseling away through the solidified basalt, that were once lava flows, for a few hundred thousand years. Parts of the Caldera and the volcanic canyon through which the river flowed were at least a million years old. I watched the water, gushing, spraying and frothing, teeming with rainbow streaks. Beyond, the forest lay dense, speckled with fall colors burning bright. I breathed in deep and finally felt at ease. I spotted a trailhead and followed it. I ended up doing a loop and then found another trail, then another. When I hike my mind becomes blank. Well not exactly blank, just lacking thought. The American-British writer Bill Bryson in his book *A Walk in the Woods* talks about how *walking like this you exist in a kind of mobile Zen mode, your brain like a balloon tethered with string, accompanying but not actually part of the body below*. I don't think I was that untethered, but I welcomed the break from the clutter of thoughts and anxieties that seemed to dominate the trip—of how I had begun to perceive a certain category of people, and worried about how I—an immigrant was perceived in return. Here, in nature, it was easier to just be, however ephemeral. I took in the scenery and kept walking. I stopped by a pond on the trail. Golden leaves rested at the water's edge, with shriveling curled edges, reaching for the autumn sun, the lily pads shedding their last petals of the season. The place looked like a poster you'd see in a meditation center.

It was midday and getting a little warmer. I made my way back and found a bench facing the waterfall. Except for one family at the parking lot, I hadn't run into another soul the whole time. I took out my sandwich—a multigrain baguette slathered with hummus, avocado, slices of crunchy red peppers, and black forest ham. I stared at the gushing water and wondered what to do next. Should I read *In Patagonia*? Should I write in my Moleskine? I lingered. I was adamant to feel the glory of solitude in this gorgeous hidden and ancient waterfall, in a place afar.

Repeating thoughts coursed through my mind of what I was trying to do, to feel. I thought about my father and our long hikes back in India. The rocky trails of low lying Garhwal hills in Uttaranchal, the rolling green slopes and the winding path through the tea gardens of Darjeeling and Nilgiris, the unmarked trails to hidden monasteries in Sikkim, the treacherous roads up Lohagad, Sinhagad, and Pratapgad fortresses in the monsoons, and our long walks on the beaches of Kannur marveling at waves as high as a four-story building. Memories from a time not that long ago but suddenly so distant. I thought about my time in Yellowstone. The sheer size of Yellowstone is overwhelming, it dwarfs everything that's in it, almost understates it—the wildlife, the geysers, the springs, the pristine lakes, the ravaged forests, the mountains, the rolling unending valleys of Hayden and Lamar, the canyons, the waterfalls, everything. My father would have enjoyed exploring it, pacified my fear of the bears by reminding me about the amphibious Bengal Tiger of Sundarbans that had jumped up our boat, snarled at us, before jumping back into the water and swimming away, while I (twenty-two at the time of that holiday) stood petrified behind my father. He would have marveled at the geysers around Old Faithful (the colorful stains of thermophiles gave some geysers magnificent colors), and appreciated the otherworldly feel of Mammoth hot springs, and the steaming Mystic falls hidden far beyond the tourist infested Biscuit Basin boardwalk, likening it to some alien planet. He would have been dismayed at the somewhat emaciated wolves of Hayden Valley and slowed the car, for pictures, every time we passed a herd of pensive bison, giant owls, and once even a big horned sheep. We would have hiked up Mt. Washburn for the spectacular 360-degree views, dotted with plumes of smoke, dew drop sized lakes, showcasing the sheer size and flora diversity of Yellowstone. We would have trudged through dense pine forest along the rolling golden grassy balds to the crystal-clear Shoshone Lake, all the while discussing what we'd do if we came upon a bear. He would've joked, "I have nothing to worry about. All I have to do is run faster than you." At that I laughed out loud, knocking me out my reverie.

    I remembered another line from the Bryson book, *Where I was, in fact, was companionless, far away from where I had gotten off the trail…* I had not gotten off the trail. I had embarked upon a new path, a path where I would not see my father for another two years. The hard realization that the distance between us wasn't just across oceans and continents but also administrative. He'd been worried that I was doing this alone, disappointed at the arduous tourist visa application process. I stretched and twirled my hair (and my thoughts), part braiding and part matting the different strands into a plait, a compulsive habit I have of playing with my hair; a mild form of Trichotillomania according to WebMd.

    In four months, on February 22, 2017, two Indian engineers drinking at a bar in a small town in Kansas would be shot at by a white male screaming "get out of my country." One of them,

Srinivas Kuchibotla would die. Six days later his wife would ask in a Facebook post: Do we belong here? I would read their profiles and life story in *The New York Times* and *Wired*, affected by the similarities of our backgrounds. My father would ask me, "Is that where you went for your trip?" I would reply, "Not even close," but then double check the geography of the state just to be sure. Life would go on. I would plan more trips and see Yosemite, Grand Canyon, Olympic National Park, and Acadia. But that uneasy feeling would never go away. All that was ahead of me.

    I continued staring at the water untangling my hair that felt like a dreadlock. I thought about Lannie. In the book, *In Patagonia*, Bruce Chatwin writes about the beauty of Patagonia and fictionalized tales of simple people with fantastical backgrounds. I tried to make one up for Lannie and imagined her sitting at this very spot with pastries in her backpack. Who was Lannie? Did I disrupt her morning? Did I provide any value to it the way she did to mine? And what about the others that I had met the past week? And what did they make of me? British born American writer Pico Iyer, wrote in his essay "Why We Travel", that sometimes we travel to shake up our complacencies. Iyer quoted the philosopher and essayist George Santayana, *We need sometimes to escape into open solitudes, into aimlessness, into the moral holiday of running some pure hazard, in order to sharpen the edge of life, to taste hardship, and to be compelled to work desperately for a moment at no matter what.* In my case, it wasn't complacency. Introversion, reticence, accent, color of my skin, immigration status, alone and outside my comfort zone—reasons and excuses I was unable to get past, shake up or off. But I was trying, and because of it I had experienced the physical manifestation of solitude, loneliness, contentment, fear, panic and epiphany in nature and its sights, and despite it all, managed to bask in the peace that came with it. And for that I was grateful. I took a deep breath in then out. In then out. I repeated the motion a few times.

I got up to leave. I was about to trash the brown paper bag when I noticed two pastries, slightly squashed and damp, at the bottom of the bag: a raspberry Danish and an apple strudel. I had not asked for those. I wondered if it had been the blue beanie lady, or perhaps Lannie. Taking in the landscape around me one more time, I smiled and devoured the pastries.

The Most Poetic Thing

by Jose Hernandez Diaz

At 6 a.m., I read Lorca's *Poema del Cante Jondo*. I take a photo
Of "La Lola" in the sunlight and post it on Facebook and Instagram.

The talented poet Dara Wier likes it. That makes my day.
Then, I submit poems to a literary magazine and prepare

My submissions for August 1st, when a few more journals open.
Also, I edit a prose poem about a dragon and a horse rider.

In the evening, when I'm finishing up some work on the computer
At the local library, an O.G. from the neighborhood with gang tattoos

Covering his body and face, walks in the library with his daughters
And helps them look for books. They tell him the names of the books

And he says "let's look for them alphabetically." I can't help but smile,
As one of the toughest guys in the barrio is in the children's section

Of the library looking for books with his kids. Much respect, though,
I keep thinking: that's the most poetic thing I've seen all day.

Black Hole Beheld

by Michael J. Leach

Distance and time melt away as we gaze in sheer wonder at your oval shape and your dazzling halo. You are the proof of Einstein's Theory of Relativity, the pure truth that's eluded artists' impressions. You are a force of nature with a heat signature, your gravitational warmth now encoded into pixels by a worldwide network of telescopes synchronised and operating to the asymptotes of perfection. Thanks to Dr Katie Bouman and her team of astronomers, physicists, mathematicians and engineers, we see you there in a galaxy as far away from Earth as 45 trillion trips between London Town and NYC. You draw in our eyes like you draw in those streams of matter swirling around you. You illuminate our eyes and our minds, fast becoming the contemporary face of astrophysics. As we look beyond your event horizon at your black core, we see a space far bigger than we are, weighing in at 4.1 billion Suns and reaching a diameter of 60 million km. Though you've been scaled down to this size that our eyes can take in, you still give us a sense of perspective – a way of seeing our place in this cosmic continuum of time and space that Einstein theorised over a hundred years ago. You are a high-resolution reconstruction brought to us by computational scientist Dr Katie Bouman. You are a force of nature with a heat signature, your gravitational warmth now encoded into pixels. Distance and time melt away as we gaze in sheer wonder at your oval shape and your dazzling halo.

This image gives us a first view of you, black hole.

Chance that Mimics Choice

by V. N. Alexander

How is anything radically new ever created in nature? Is it true, as some scientists say, that everything under the sun is just a different arrangement of the same old materials that have existed since the dawn of the universe? Are poems just different permutations of ideas that have been expressed before?

    I was a freshman student of literature and budding novelist when I started to wonder about such things, and I was eventually led—following the example of Vladimir Nabokov, who was a butterfly scientist as well as a novelist—to pursue a course of study that would combine narrative theory, poetics, physics, and evolution. The title of this essay is a quote from a short story by Nabokov, "The Vane Sisters" (1959), in which a once-mentioned character—an eccentric librarian named Porlock—likes to search through old books looking for typos that might transform a sentence into one with an entirely new and different meaning: "the chance that mimics choice, the flaw that looks like a flower." Porlock's friend, Cynthia Vane, suspects that such "chance" typos might be messages from ghosts, who—because they are immaterial and unable to affect material reality—are left merely to tinker with the probabilities that determine chance events.

Occasionally, Nabokov liked to toy with the idea of the supernatural, possibly because an intervening spirit is the analog of an intervening author. Clearly gods are, and always have been, created in the image of the artist. According to the events as literally depicted in "The Vane Sisters," there is no such thing as ouija-board-style interpolations of supernatural forces in the real world; however, the astute (or superstitious) reader may find the hidden acrostic in the last paragraph that spells out a message from the by-then departed souls of Cynthia and her sister Sybil. This proves to the reader that there is an all-knowing entity above and beyond the reality of the narrative who can hide meta-narrative clues to make one suspect His existence. All beliefs in gods, ghosts, angels, devils or spirits are based upon reading the world as if it were a work of art, interpreting coincidental patterns as if they were intentional. I don't consider Nabokov superstitious, but I do think he believed in his own god-like power to create.

My research over the past twenty years or so has enabled me to confirm that, yes, truly new things do emerge in the world. Authors can create. While working on a PhD in English focusing on narrative theory and the philosophy of science, I became a visiting researcher at the Santa Fe Institute to study deterministic chaos, self-organization, artificial life, and the complexity sciences—new scientific concepts and tools that were being used to re-examine the question of whether or not genuine novelty can emerge, almost like a miracle, from a rearrangement of already existing parts. It was said that "effectual factors" in a non-linear (complex) system is what allows the system to self-organize, become complex.

But what does that mean?!

The physicists I was working with at the time weren't able to provide an answer to that question in a way that satisfied me, so

I kept asking. Eventually, I came to land in a new sub-field called biosemiotics. I now understand that these "effectual factors" are the qualities of relationships between physical things that can't be quantified. Similarity is analog and relative. So is proximity. How near and how similar something is to something else may affect the probability of a new relationship crystalizing. Effectual factors are like literary puns and coincidental patterns. For example, a moth that happens to be resting on a tree trunk of a similar color to itself inadvertently furthers its own chances of survival. To a bird cruising by, the dull moth looks like bark. Coincidental intersections of similar things may form a pattern that can be interpreted by some living being and these moments are points at which the strict determinists, like a Pierre Laplace or a Daniel Dennett, will see predictable trajectories of matter and energy take an unpredictably sharp turn. Every artist I have ever known describes the process of creative discovery in a similar fashion.

But much less obvious is the kind of creative interpretations that go on in nature even when there is no intelligent animal to interpret the coincidence. All living systems tend to interpret coincidences, and this is how they get their power of self-organization, how they hold together better than you'd think possible, how they come to function in advantageous ways far beyond what the numbers might predict. My particular role within the field of biosemiotics is to explore how all semiosis (i.e., the purposeful, self-confirming habits) always begins with the radically transformative process of poesis. I have found that every new semiotic habit (rule-bound biological process) must begin as a mistaken interpretation of a coincidental pattern. For example, the wrong molecule happens to fit into a cell receptor, and this causes a chain of reactions that repurpose that receptor for some other function. Chance that mimics choice. Adaptation always involves a typo, a mutation, an error, that gets mistaken for something else. This must be so, for the only way to respond to something foreign and new is to mistake it for something we do know, assimilate it into ourselves and allow it to change ourselves. Think of the proto-eukaryotic single-cell organism that ingested another single-cell organism it took to be a tasty meal. The ingested but not digested organism was assimilated and became the nucleus of eukaryotic cells which eventually gave rise to all fungi, plants and animals, you, and me. That's a pretty amazing invention based on a mistaken interpretation.

Human language emerged from such semiotic biological processes. Basic semiosis, far from being unique to humans, primates or other higher animals, is co-extensive with life. I enjoy working in biosemiotics because it offers a much-needed bridge between the sciences and the arts. One of my driving motivations has always been to show that the literary arts are useful to the sciences and the sciences are useful to the arts. The humanities have suffered, as much as the sciences have, from the wedge that has been driven between art and science, subjective and objective, mind and matter.

It's my creative work as a novelist and a narrative-poet that has given me insight into the natural creativity of evolutionary processes and pattern formation. Creative writers know better than scientists how truly radical new ideas can emerge in language, as the result of some poetic interpretation. Artists tend to be aware of the way subconscious processes innovate, not through logical laws or relationships, but often though coincidences. Life uses language-like processes, and, conversely, a poet can create radically new ideas using biosemiotic-like processes.

The world is alive with meaning; nature itself uses metaphor and metonymy in its creations. When things are coincidentally like each other (metaphoric) or coincidentally near each other (metonymic) this can constrain the way they interact and may affect the probabilities of certain causal outcomes. I believe that this is what underlies self-organization in nature and what makes it seem "purposeful," as if some whimsical artist were behind it all. This is a sense of purposeful nature that is very different from a religious or spiritual notion, such as Wordsworth had for example, one that relies instead upon ecological and semiotic notions. Nature truly is a self-creating work of art.

Andromeda

by Martha McCollough

a little star becomes a starry wheel
        rolling in huge silence   toward us
announced by meteoric children
        flashing to nobody's rescue
the catastrophe
will be continuous
        too big to be felt

thinking   *I don't want to*
the bride approaches glittering
        speechless

later she'll wonder   must every
        wedding be a bloodbath

spidersilk plus cosmic debris equals
    cobweb   veil of andromeda
    spiraling from interplanetary cloud
        into her room
brightly particulate
in slanted light
   dust in the clouded eye
        of told you so
eye that sees
   mother trail bright waves
       across her wrist   *no one*
          more beautiful   all mothers

say these things   but mother not
where the gods can hear

that's how you end up wheeling
    upside down   through heaven
        nailed to your glittery throne

• • •

clink of chains
andromeda's monster rises
    where the sea roars & whitens
        time for the sacred wedding
or feast
perhaps the god thinks
it will be a treat for him

but what can he do, Cetus
   with this little breathing thing
      finless   earthy   no part
        of his usual diet

someone should ask if he might rather
     sink   silent as the bride
       into the starless deep

• • •

   already andromeda
  shone like a dropped
     earring
    over the departures
     of certain huge animals
   slow-moving   dusty as old rugs

leaving a remnant bitterness
   of wild cousins   missing
      their phantom familiars
osage orange   honeylocust   coffeetree
   all this puzzling unsweetness
      is only fidelity to extinct
         desire   the austere preference
           of vanished monsters
apple will you grow bitter
   without your bees
      your bears   gorging on windfall
      in abandoned orchards
what is a word for
   animals that wish

• • •

she wishes to have
a serious belief in the timely approach
   of the winged bridegroom
      spiraling down
      meteoric flash of his shield
eyes closed   waving the fatal head
   he'll say don't look
      and she won't

Erinys

by Martha McCollough

Be in the world
for me while
I sleep

do you hear
that voice
outsmarting
itself again

saying saying
makes it so

send a green fly
to annoy
send a black fly
for torment

from your cave
doorway to hell
my heart
or whatever

hell of boredom
or lake of fire

MARTHA MCCOLLOUGH

in which
love falls
apart
click click
nothing

a girl considers
the history
of love

how
there is so little
of it

humming black
cloud in the shape
& place of me

be in the world
visit his sleep

unfold sudden
shadowed
wings

Circus Lights

by Franklin Einspruch

FRANKLIN EINSPRUCH

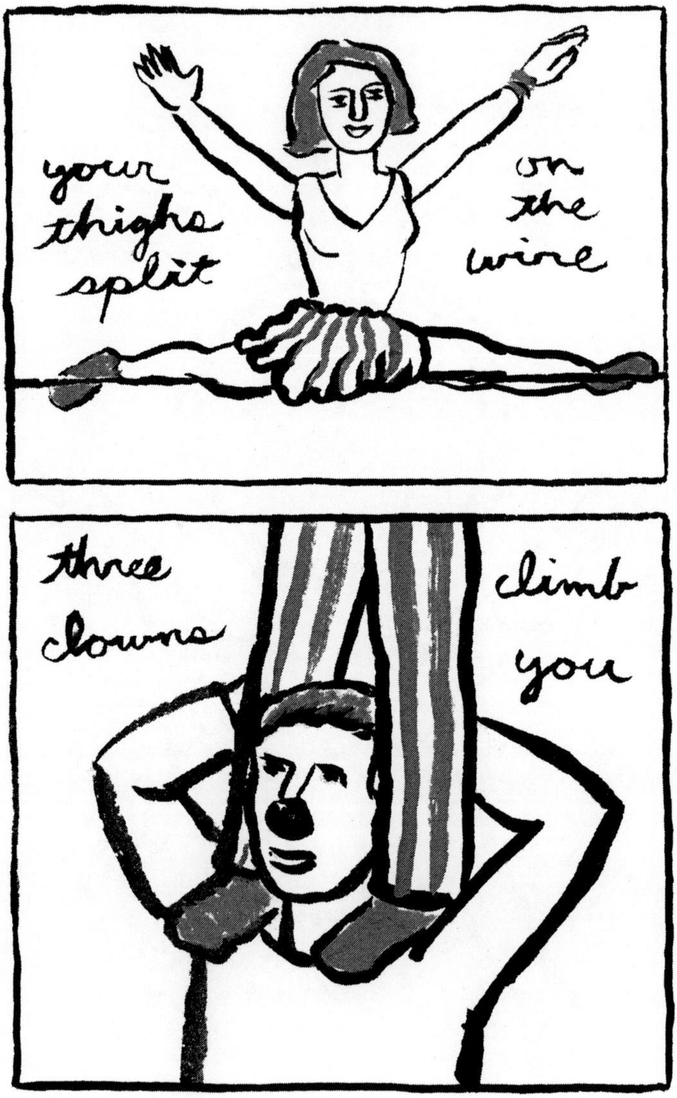
your thighs split
on the wire
three clowns
climb you

FRANKLIN EINSPRUCH

the hardest trick remains watching the glow

FRANKLIN EINSPRUCH

Longing

by Christie Marra

Ernie and Sue said nothing as they drove the dark, curving road to the hospital. Sue stared out the window trying to ignore the baby's cries, but finally she gave in, leaning her head down to rub the baby's wispy hair with her nose. As Sue inhaled her baby's smell, she felt at home. For the first time since her daddy died, she belonged to someone. And her baby girl belonged to her. But not for long. *Turn around!* she wanted to cry, to make Ernie turn and drive as fast as he could out of town and across state lines, to somewhere they could live and work and watch their baby grow up. Instead, she lifted her head, rolled the window down and sucked in the damp night air, hoping it would chase away the longing inside her.

The entire time Sue had squatted on the floor of the gas station bathroom she stared at the graffiti on the wall next to the sink. "Sally loves Johnny 4eva" the red writing declared. She had just enough time to wonder if Sally still loved Johnny before the next pain came. Even though Sue felt like her body might break apart right where her legs met, she didn't scream. She took the wet rag and bit down hard on it. Her top teeth missed the rag and dug into her lip, drawing blood. Sue found the taste comforting.

"Sally loves Johnny 4eva," Sue read again, and this time when the pain came it seemed different, and when she reached down between her legs she felt something coming, sticky and wet, hard and curved. She pushed hard and held her arms in front of the spot where her body was opened. She screamed. She screamed so loud she shook the walls. She screamed and pushed and pushed again and it all started coming out, the baby with its dark hair just like Ernie's, covered with blood and grime.

Sue had leaned back onto the cement floor, grateful for its coolness, and put the baby on her chest, holding it with one arm and trying to wipe the messiness off it with the other. She took special care to clear the gook out of its nose and throat just like the internet said. When she had wiped off as much as she could, she took the scissors she'd snuck from Mama's kitchen drawer and cut the rubbery cord attached to the baby with trembling hands, getting as close as she dared to its stomach. Even though she knew she'd never have to see it, Sue didn't want her baby growing up with an outie.

She held the naked baby against her, watching its head move back and forth, its tiny mouth open. The baby started to cry so loudly Sue expected to see Ernie burst into the bathroom in alarm. It seemed to be searching for something, pushing its nose and little O mouth repeatedly onto Sue's sweatshirt. She felt a strange sensation in her breasts, and realized her body was reacting to the baby's search. Her baby was hungry, and her body responded, and she wondered if she should let the baby nurse, just this once, to give it a good chance to start off healthy. But as she brought the baby up under her shirt Sue felt something else creeping up inside her, a different sensation that made her worry that if she let the baby suck that pre-milk from her it would know she was its mother, and it would get scared and cry more when she did what she had to do. She pulled the baby out from under her shirt and wiped it off again with one of the two towels she'd brought, then wrapped it in the other. More than anything, she longed to put the baby on her breast, not only to quiet it but also because she knew it would be the only chance she would have to nurse it.

"What is it?" Ernie asked as soon as Sue got into the car, but Sue just shook her head.

"No sense in both of us knowin'," she told Ernie. "If we talk about it, just say IT. If you say 'him' or 'her', folks will figure it out." Sue had spent the last few months dressing in baggy sweaters and sweats instead of the size one jeans and extra small tops she usually wore. She'd eaten extra helpings at dinner so Mama would understand why she was getting fat, even early on when more often than not the extra helpings didn't stay down very long. Good thing she had a bush beneath her bedroom window to catch the extra helpings when they came back up.

Sue couldn't let Ernie blow it now, especially when she had only a few more months until she left this hick town for college. No doubt if Ernie knew they had a little girl baby, it wouldn't be long before somebody else in town knew they had a little girl baby, and not long after that her mama would know they had a little girl baby, and Sue would have to say goodbye to college before she even said hello.

"Park over there in the corner," Sue directed Ernie as he pulled into the hospital parking lot. The corner of the lot was empty and the light in that section was out. Nobody would notice Ernie sitting in the parked car, no matter how long he had to wait.

Sue walked away from the car as slowly as she could, hugging her hidden baby closer to her chest. She kept her head up, trying to avoid the sweet smell of the baby's head, which was just about the best thing she had ever smelled, even better than the eucalyptus bath soap Mama had brought her back from Richmond last Christmas. Sue felt the tears starting. Maybe she *could* just be a mama… She shook her head and forced her tired legs to take her to the hospital faster. Sue knew she couldn't smell her baby's head again.

As she approached the ER doors, Sue started to shake. What if the nurses wouldn't take the baby? What if the new law she'd read about, the one that let you leave your newborn at the hospital and walk away without giving your name, wasn't true? Maybe the story was a hoax like that *War of the Worlds* radio broadcast she'd learned about in history class. Would the nurses call the police on her? Then Mama'd call Sue a slut and a criminal and she'd never let her go to college! There was, however, a tiny part of her that hoped the newspaper story was a lie, because then she'd *have to* keep the baby to keep from ending up in jail.

Sue kept her eyes up and focused on the red letters above the doors, making sure she didn't look down at her baby. Her legs quivered.

"Hello," a voice said from the bench beside the entrance.

Sue jumped back a little.

"I didn't mean to startle you," the woman said. "I just wondered why you're taking the baby into the hospital."

Sue looked at the woman, a tall, thin shadow in the dark, and she stepped back again, instinctively lowering her face to the baby's head. She inhaled deeply and closed her eyes, and she saw herself with her baby and Ernie, far from the hospital and from her mama, holding each other and laughing.

"This may sound crazy but, by any chance are you taking the baby to…to…" The woman stopped speaking.

Sue stood very still, wanting the woman to leave so she could go into the hospital and do the thing she came to do. Quickly. She didn't know how much longer she could hold her baby before loving her too much to let her go.

The woman stepped toward Sue into the patch of light in front of the ER entrance. She had dark smudges under her eyes and wrinkled clothes and Sue wondered if she was homeless. She trembled and hugged the baby even closer, and as the baby's nose met her breast she felt the liquid begin to flow. She started to turn away, toward where Ernie waited in the car.

"If you're giving your baby…"

Sue turned back toward the woman, and the woman paused for what seemed like a very long time. She reached her trembling hand toward the baby bundled against Sue's chest.

"If you're giving your baby to the nurses," she said finally, "maybe I can help you."

Sue backed away a few steps, fighting the desire to turn away and put the baby to her breast. "What do you want?"

"A baby," the woman's voice cracked. "A baby of my own. But I'm forty-two years old. I'm divorced. I don't have enough money to pay for artificial insemination. And do you know"… The woman took a deep breath. "Do you know how long a person has to wait to adopt a newborn?"

Sue backed away a little more. The baby was moving her head around against Sue's chest and Sue felt her body pushing out more milk. "What do you want?" she asked again.

"I…I'm a lawyer and I know when new laws get passed. I know that when you take it in there," she gestured to the hospital, "social services will get her. And I know I can do a better job raising a baby than someone chosen by social services. I figured, maybe…maybe you would see that I'll be a good mother and give me a chance."

Sue turned her back to the woman. How could she trust a woman who was just waiting outside the hospital hoping someone would give her a baby? This was crazy! Wasn't it? Was it? Sue started to walk toward the hospital doors, but then got scared again. What if somebody who knew Mama happened to be in the ER with a bloody face or a broken leg right when she went in to give her baby up? They'd for sure tell Mama and there was no way she would let Sue go off to college if she knew Sue'd had a baby. She would end up losing both her baby and her chance to go to college and escape this little nothing town where all the women ended up old and mean before they reached fifty, just like Mama. Would it be better to let this unknown woman take her baby than take her inside and risk being recognized?

Sue held the baby out in front of her so she could see its face with its miniature mouth and nose. The baby opened its eyes wide. Sue wondered whether her baby would remember her if they ever crossed paths. Of the two of them only Sue would look about the same as she did right now. Sue swallowed hard to keep from crying.

She turned back around to face the woman.

"I promise I'll be good to her," the woman said softly.

Sue nodded, burying her nose in the baby's whispy hair one last time. She handed the baby to the woman and turned away quickly. The brief sight of the woman holding her baby was already more than she wanted to see.

Sue ran to the car.

"How'd it go?" Ernie asked, jiggling his leg up and down against the keys dangling from the ignition. The tinny noise hurt Sue's head.

"Fine." Sue climbed into the passenger seat and turned her back to Ernie. She leaned her forehead against the cold window and closed her eyes, hoping Ernie wouldn't notice the tears on her cheeks. Ernie didn't seem to notice because he kept right on jiggling his stupid leg and making stupid noises with his stupid keys.

"Did the nurses ask you questions? Did you have to give your name or anything?" Ernie's voice rose in pitch, and Sue swallowed a sob. She wished Ernie would be quiet. She closed her eyes and pictured the wide lawn in front of the columned buildings and the professors with their funny jackets and glasses. But the longing welled up again and more tears fell.

"Did they say anything?"

Sue wished he would stop asking questions. She just wanted to be quiet and hide her crying.

"Well…" Ernie said. "What did they---?"

"Shut up!" Sue shouted.

Ernie grunted loudly as he revved the engine and exited the parking lot, but he didn't say another word the entire way back to Sue's house.

He stopped the car in front of the house, and Sue left the car quickly without so much as a goodbye. She knew by the way Ernie spun his wheels pulling out of her driveway that she had made him angry, but she didn't care. She hoped she'd never see him again.

Sue darted into the darkness between her house and the neighbor's, pulled off her bloody clothes and threw them into the neighbor's trash can. She crept in her side door and headed to her bed, weaving her way around the empty beer cans and the overflowing ash trays and the ripped recliners where her mama and step dad lay snoring.

Up Close

by Jennifer Markell

A dandelion's fruiting head
a jeweled amphora.
Spinach tissue's blue
mosaic, too beautiful to eat.
Stomata dot the skin of trillium
like points on a map, what's laid bare
by a microscope: a pine needle's thirst
seen at the infection site where
brown fungus burrows
through a season's drought.
For now, the lobed algae live on,
traveling in pairs,
and pollen grains gather on anthers.
Tucked inside the feathers
of whistling ducks,
diatoms gorge on sunlight.

It's hard to get a bead on god
by Jennifer Markell

Sometimes I try belief like a hat,
tilting to see how things appear
under a brim. Run my finger
along the edge of a hollow & stride
through presbyopic alleys
haloed by faith. Sometimes

I rest on a hard bench with the atheists.
Darwin & Marx, Simone de Beauvoir.
We consider the transcendent hand
of evolution. The siren song of paradise.
Goethe drops by to say if there's a god,
it's time to review the plan.

Avisaurus fly in & out of my dreams.
For every answer, a thousand questions
expand as our time on earth recedes.
I sing in the shower. Janis & Aretha join me
in the space between words.
Aretha looks divine in her feathered hat.

Ends Meet

by Alex Wells Shapiro

Our apartment must hold
enough people to work off
the cost of living. We lower

our shoulders to a brick each, backs
huddled like linemen, anchor
our hips, push and repeat,

our thrusts incremental
and abraising against
the coarse exposure,

our outward scrum aiming
at studs shelled by sparse
décor. After

our exhaust, husks folding
and crumbling, a new roommate
wedges in to work toward further expansion

of our space.
The neighbors geyser through the walls,
piling and mingling in a passive mosh pit,
and everyone fits.

The Secret Life of An Old Maine Shoe
by Christina Marsden Gillis

The shoe didn't fit, but its worn condition told me that it had fit someone once, some woman to be more exact; but that was probably about 140 years ago. Since then it had remained nestled in the plaster in the westward facing upstairs bedroom wall, just to the left of the window that looks out to the sea. I know that bedroom, the one where my husband and I brought an infant child who is now a father of college-age children; I know the house, and I know the Maine island where I have spent every summer of my adult life. But the shoe was a mystery.

A contractor installing new windows last summer discovered it. With it came the uncanny sense that each year, when I returned to my home in California, a secret sharer, a spirit unknown to me, took possession of our house, one of only six that remain of a village settled in 1789. On an island depopulated in 1930 and now a winter ghost town, the woman who once wore that shoe was keeping watch.

She may have been looking out for witches and other evil spirits prone to home invasion; or perhaps she feared the strange serpents and marine creatures described by the Federal Writers Project in their 1937 account of superstitious belief in Maine. More likely, the shoe could have been protecting the household against more tangible dangers: those posed by the sea itself to a coastal fishing community (Daniel Gott, founder of the island community, was drowned, with his two sons, in 1814), to say nothing of the ever-present threats of illness or fire. The shoe was a primitive form of insurance.

So suggests the index of shoe discoveries located at the municipal museum in Northampton, England, once a site of shoe production. The listing now includes some 2000 examples, mainly in the UK, but also from Europe and North America; the earliest was at Winchester Cathedral in 1308. For 700 years, according to the index, people have been concealing shoes in walls, floors, and chimneys, and yet there exists no known first-hand written account of why.

Superstitions are powerful, and they travel. Historians tell us that a majority of the highly religious–and superstitious–early Puritan arrivals in Massachusetts, including the region around Gloucester, came from East Anglia, a region noted for both belief in witchcraft and instances of shoe concealments. Several generations later, Gloucester was the source of an emigration north to Mount Desert Island. And from there, the Gott family went on to settle their own island just off the southwest edge of Mount Desert. Our house, though built later, with an addition (where the shoe was found) later still, sits on property deeded from Daniel Gott to a son in 1812.

As for who placed the shoe in the wall, and what may have been the motivation, my best guess–and it is a guess–is a neighbor and local carpenter who was living on Gotts Island as of 1879. But like superstition itself, nothing is concrete except the shoe, its cracks and creases tracing the foot of the woman who once wore it. I am in touch with a human presence here.

Was she Susan, the wife of the neighbor builder? Or perhaps Caddie, wife of the owner of the house in 1879? I try to imagine her: the woman who presided over the domestic space of the house, who stood before the Empress Atlantic wood stove just as I do, peered out the kitchen windows to the cemetery down the hill and the dangerous ocean beyond, thinking of family and fellow islanders whose graves she can almost see. She was the protector of the household. I catch glimpses of her in the fiction of writer Ruth Moore, who grew up in our house and famously chronicled Maine island life. More than this, I cannot know. But I feel a connection. This is the power that the shoe sustains.

It sits now in a finely crafted shadow box against a background of sage green silk that brings out the color in the grommets through which the woman would have drawn up the laces. Certainly the shoe is transformed in its new setting, propped up temporarily on a table in a mid-century California house whose westward-facing windows look out to the Golden Gate. But the spirit of the woman who wore this narrow, once-elegant shoe is out of place here. In July, when we head to Maine again, we will return her, her shoe, and its inexplicable history to the house and the island where they belong, hopefully to protect our family from whatever evil forces may turn up to threaten us.

The Joy of Agony

by Mark Halpern

I am paid every month to be a 72-year-old woman. Though the payment is only on paper, so is her mode of expression. She is, in British parlance, an "agony aunt."

Dear Granny Gaijin

My name is Nathan and I am a gaijin. I haven't committed a stupid-gaijin act in nearly 48 hours.

That form of opening – modeled on how television shows have led me to believe people introduce themselves at Alcoholics Anonymous meetings – is mandatory for all supplicants. In case you don't know, *gaijin* is Japanese for foreigner.

Without those opening words, letters don't get a reply and certainly don't get published. Except that if a letter is extraordinarily good, I myself insert the requisite opening – which is no more intrusively corruptive than the rest of my peculiar editing. Artistic license and all that. Why begrudge me the joy of taking charge in

| 157

the one area of my life where I can fully do so? And if I don't get enough proper letters for my column, I just write some myself.

> Yesterday I picked up my weekly load from the dry cleaner's, but I could see that a button had gone missing from one of my "Y shirts" (why do they call dress shirts that?). This is the second time. I told the clerk and got a blank stare. When I asked that they sew on a new button, she said it would take fifteen days and they'd charge 378 yen. They already make a ton of money from me. Also, the only other dry cleaner's in my neighbourhood is even worse.
> What's up? I thought Japanese stores always gave pretty good service.
>
> *Nat from Nashville*

It's harder to reply to the letters I've written myself, perhaps because I'm uncertain there's even one person curious for my answer. Without raw curiosity – coming mainly in the shape of voyeurism – all is lost. But I try. This is not some great literary enterprise, where the narrator-hero's frail nobility is revealed tiptoe by graceful tiptoe along a fine high-wire of delicate words, his arms outstretched right and left to give balance just as they fend off the brutalizing forces – some personal, some impersonal – that define a fate we're all duty-bound to flee. That I leave for another day.

> *Dear Nathaniel,*
>
> Several decades ago, a young foreigner of my acquaintance politely asked a Japanese dry cleaner's to replace a button and they responded, "we do not offer that service." He then told them angrily that they therefore should not offer the service of tearing off buttons. You

may try saying something of that nature, but smart-alecky talk will surely earn you nothing but another blank stare. Unlike other shops here, dry cleaner's mostly – how might I put this delicately? – suck rotten eggs.

You seem like a nice young man who probably wears Y-shirts every day to a fancy job that pays oodles more money than is earned by an old pensioner like me. So I suggest you patronize one of the harrowingly expensive dry cleaner's near the majestic office tower where you work. They tend to leave buttons intact. You can go during your obscenely long lunch break or perhaps just improperly burden your pretty, young secretary with this non-employment-related task.

Also, Y-shirts are so called because: (1) in olden days, men's dress shirts were always white; (2) "Y" is pronounced like the middle two syllables of ho-wa-i-to, the local four-syllable local pronunciation of "white;" (3) "Y-shirt" is reminiscent of "T-shirt"; and (4) Japanese schools do not specifically teach that "T" can denote a shape.

Gran

The Cayman Islands-incorporated publisher of *Living Better Than Others – Tokyo* is a public relations-advertising-educational-translation business with diverse ventures in Japan. In consideration of assorted monthly duties, which extend well beyond Granny's literary efforts, my contract stipulates that I be paid $2,600 per month, all of which is formally allocated towards my employment as a "full time journalist." After deducting the portion that is not actually paid, as well as expenses and a kickback to the editor, I retain $1,100. Of this, I would, were I an economist, notionally allocate *positive $1,500* to my freelance website maintenance business and *negative $400* to Granny. But thanks to her, the Ministry of Foreign Affairs has issued me a Foreign Press Registration Card, which is worth its weight in ether. It improves my life multifariously – including, especially, my fantasy life.

> *… I am a sexy, beautiful Japanese woman in my early twenties. Presently, I am being hit upon by a gentle-mannered, though somewhat physically-unappealing, foreign guy. Although he has a degree in comparative literature from an Ivy League university, where he studied on a scholarship, people seem to regard him as a loser and he lacks most of the usual hallmarks of credibility. However, he does possess an FPR Card. Should I trust him? …*

Dear Shikibu-san

Apologies, my pet, but I only give advice to gaijin.

Gran

Some other benefits of my writing job: (1) I can truthfully present myself in society as a professional, salaried "social commentator" whose monthly column appears under a pseudonym in a broadly-read magazine, which claim is backed up when necessary by my written contract ("broadly" here indicating diversity, rather than numerousness, of the readership); (2) I experience the overblown satisfaction of being a published writer; (3) I may air my complaints about Japanese society in print and even bleat away at nature's harsh and unrelenting oppression of man;

> ... *How come so many public toilets here still don't provide hand soap? Or, like most Starbucks in Tokyo, they seldom refill their soap dispensers and take months to repair them when they break? My Japanese girlfriend doesn't seem to think this is a problem, insisting that she and her compatriots still maintain a completely sanitary existence. And while we're on the subject, how come women use approximately one hundred and thirty times more toilet paper than men? What is it you women actually do in the toilet that is so different? ...*

Dear Atticus

As to the lack of soap, many Japanese people are not as clean as they think. But I cast no such aspersions on your girlfriend. Perhaps she is simply, like some Japanese, unable to tolerate any suggestion from a foreigner that even one subatomic particle is out of place in their flawless biosphere.

As to what women actually do in the toilet, we are not permitted to reveal that mystery to men.

Gran

and (4) I get to air my complaints about other foreigners.

... I haven't committed a stupid-gaijin act in over two weeks. Since moving to Japan early this year [blah blah blah] ...

Dear Holden

Having moved here so recently, you doubtless engage in stupid-gaijin behaviour daily without realizing it. Wake up and conduct olfactory detection of the coffee.

Gran

As to my explanation about "Y Shirts," I just made it up; yet I think it's probably all true. And while the slovenly use of the English language by many *gaijin* certainly disentitles them from complaining about its abuse by the Japanese, I've nonetheless permitted the latter to become a recurring theme.

... I have back home a certain maiden aunt who is graced with the type of gentility of spirit that can only be engendered by a highly sheltered upbringing. Last week, this sweet, silver-haired angel, whom I hold very dear, visited Tokyo for the first time. Her own character being like that of a rose lovingly tended in a glass-walled conservatory, I decided to escort her to a flower arrangement exhibition in Shinjuku. Afterwards, we went to a tea salon that, from the outside, looked entirely respectable, where we waited fifteen minutes in line. Finally, we reached the reception counter, only to confront a large sign proclaiming, "We now provide S&M at your table."

Needless to say, we departed instantly. But this was mortifying all round. How might I avoid such unpleasantness in the future?

Dora from Delaware

Dear Eudora

Among many other duties, the good hostess must forewarn guests from abroad simply to ignore all English words proffered by restaurants. Menu descriptions in particular – "sir-fried galaxius maculatus with assorted mold," "greasy sticks wrapped in lousewort," "pork with ears of brown fleg" – may be as misleading as they are off-putting.

By contrast, in Japan general appearances are highly reliable. As to the particular tea shop sign that caused your discomfiture, I believe it was likely intended to alert patrons to a newly-introduced offering of Siggersfield & Martinson brand fine jams with the shop's high tea service.

These jams are, by the way, a lovely treat.

Gran

My readers – many of whom know Tokyo better than I – neither expect nor desire accuracy. The very best letters they send are as imaginative as Granny's replies. But though she makes up all the details, she still speaks truth. As to restaurants, while the real me usually packs my own bento lunch or eats at cheap chain shops, I occasionally splurge. And when visiting client offices in Ginza or Nihonbashi, I often poke my head into the higher-class eateries to check out their English menus. Also, I have lots of time available, owing to the fact that I don't work very hard. So in addition to my admittedly-imperfect knowledge of things Japanese, I have a well-educated imagination and enough leisure to allow it free rein.

That being so, and I being a weak, wretched, troubled and un-appreciated creature, I often fantasize about what I *should have done* in some or other challenging circumstance. What I *would have done*, that is, had I not been me. What I *will do* once I have the confidence and power that come from advancing one's position in society. Meanwhile, the writing process requires a focus and precision that lets me lose myself in fantasy – that lets fantasy utterly overwhelm memory. I am left all puffed up, though it is a transient satisfaction.

> *… The typhoon passed, but the re-ticketing was chaos. So I just returned to the platform and jumped on the next uncrowded train heading back to Tokyo, figuring to find an unoccupied seat once everyone else had boarded. Though I tried staying out of the way pending that resolution, I somehow found myself blocking a slick-haired, shiny-shirted Japanese guy in his forties from instantly accessing his seat. He was probably agitated by the train's delay, but that cannot excuse his coarse rudeness. Although his venture at human speech – an aggregation of disjointed syllables rendered into Osaka dialect – was mostly incomprehensible, I gathered that he expected an obsequious, sniveling apology. I declined to give him satisfaction. I, too, was justifiably agitated by the delay.*

Some minutes later, the uncouth lout made his way down the car to where I'd next planted myself, delivered a few more incoherent utterances, and stood there scowling. I rose from my seat, flexed my muscles tight, and brought my body extremely close to his. He continued to scowl and grunt, but was otherwise motionless. Nonetheless, I shouted in Japanese, firmly, forcefully and at slow, even tempo, "How dare you strike me! Everyone here is a witness! Get your pathetic self back to your seat and sit down and shut up, or I'll have the police on you! I have already taken your photo with my cell phone and posted it on www.offensive-brutes.com."

This strategy was 100% effective. But later my friend said the guy might have been yakuza, so I should have just debased myself in apology and then hid away in another car as unobtrusively as possible …

Dear Lancelot

Brilliant. I applaud your manly courage and nimble, creative intellect.

Gran

But it's not all self-indulgence. There is a true public-service element. I really do explain how we foreigners must go about conducting our daily lives if we are to live harmoniously in this country.

… I write on a topic already canvassed extensively by Miss Manners, Ann Landers and Dear Abby, but wonder whether special considerations might apply for Japan. I have been invited to a wedding celebration for a Japanese friend. When I asked her mother what sort of gift might be useful, I was shocked at her recommendation that I bring cash. A specific sum was mentioned, making the mother seem even more vulgar. Is there any chance I am wrong to think this way? …

Dear Flannery

Yes.

Gran

It's not necessarily my inability to find a rewarding full-time position in corporate Japan – ever since an early-career debacle – that keeps me freelance. Currently, my paid endeavours include not just website maintenance and related grunt work, but also copywriting for a few Japanese tourism businesses. So I am, truly, a professional writer. Further, the modesty of my overall income is justified by the hours left available to work on the great undertaking that is my first novel. For the moment, though, Granny Gaijin provides my sole opportunity to leave a literary footprint on our sometimes muddy, sometimes dusty, often cold and lonely planet. And several years back, before the internet had blown away the glossy print editions of *Living Better Than Others* everywhere but Tokyo, my stronger efforts were often reproduced in hard copy for readers in Jakarta, Kuala Lumpur and Ho Chi Minh City – though without additional remuneration. Usually, these were stories about career opportunities, which, given the movement of Westerners within the Asia-Pacific region, have always been hot.

Dear Granny Gaijin

... early last year I accepted employment at a major Japanese company as their first foreigner permanent employee (mere technical specialists aside) ... arranged through a well-placed family friend ... I was already perfectly fluent in Japanese and ... possessed a double-first from Oxford, where I read ... many obscene exaggerations ... some staff resented my presence from the start ... and the situation worsened steadily ... after eighteen months I was sacked ... this ... blatant discrimination of the most egregious kind ... left me no choice but to institute a lawsuit ...

Fortescue-Roy from Framlingham

Dear Fauntleroy

Owing to space limitations, I have not reproduced your letter in entirety. Yet I am uncertain whether the nineteen single-spaced pages comprising its main body and itemizing the relentless victimization inflicted by your cruel Japanese masters, nor the booklet of end notes detailing and cross-referencing the relevance of each subclause of Japan's Labour Standards Law, would in any event necessarily convey to our readers a proper account of your situation. To do so requires balance.

Noting that you have already cast aside the offer of a generous termination package in favour of delivering your fate into the fat, grasping, grub-picking, oleaginous fingers of lawyers – presumably relying on some esoteric principle of Old World ethics to justify diverting your family's wealth toward funding the exorbitant legal fees necessary for a battle against a corporate giant to vindicate your besmirched honour – I think you are not actually seeking my advice. Let me thus just comment on a few particulars. I emphasize that the points touched on below are not more problematic than the others raised in your unabridged letter.

First, your nonstop sarcastic criticism of senior executives' poor English pronunciation, though accurate, was likely unhelpful and certainly embarrassing to them. And perhaps that karaoke singer did not "want to hold your hand;" perhaps the old gentleman, likely being neither Jewish nor Muslim, actually "wore a holy ham."

Second, the degree conferred by your elite university is not a license to crash "old boys" gatherings of colleagues who studied elsewhere. Also, some people achieve distinction at work merely through effort and accomplishment.

Third, your demand for wages based on each and every hour spent on company premises does not accord with customary business practices. In Japan, one is simply not paid for "voluntary overtime," even when such is undertaken out of pressure to conform for the sake of career advancement.

Fourth, repeatedly using the office microwave to warm up goat cheese sandwiches is a bad idea anywhere. The complaints do not constitute discrimination on the basis of ethnic origin. You are the guilty party. You have committed sume-hara, "smell harassment,"

against your more delicately-sensibilitied co-workers.
As to Japanese social norms, one need not fully embrace all of them. But if one chooses to live here one must accept them, even when at odds with Japan's own formal laws and regulations. Foreigners before you have made similar errors, but the follies of extreme youth are to be forgiven if one can mend his ways. Good luck, dearie.

Gran

And I really do spend most of my free hours slogging away at my novel. It's a coming-of-age story, featuring a struggle to regain lost purity. It will be my vindication and my redemption. I am more than half way through.

Johnnie Redding

by Justin Danzy

News said he died of a cocaine overdose
in the elevator shaft of an old warehouse.

He languished there for months, they said,
under a layer of ice until authorities came

and sawed him out. I wonder if I ever met him,
this Johnnie, passed by him on the street,
gave him a few singles that he used to buy a coney dog.

Maybe he hated coney dogs and bought a grilled
chicken pita instead. Maybe Johnnie had been
a construction worker, or basketball coach,

won a championship or two in the local rec league
where he preached fundamentals--hard defense
and ball movement--like his coach taught him

when he was young. Johnnie, who was never the star,
but played the right way. Johnnie, who fell on hard times,

slipped up, like Darius with the DUI, Bob with his temper,
me with the cheating and cheating and cheating again.

I want to know his face, Johnnie, but can only see his feet,
the rest of him dug up only to show
how the body rots into spectacle, how the white

of his tube socks glistened against the black ice.

Legacy

by Mary-Kim Arnold

to let their blood

                    drain over me

This is something that nobles do   and I

am descended

                from a long line of royalty

Commerce prospers   We are not afraid

of advancing armies   Rabbit blood is warm and thin

I was fully clothed when I began the rabbit ritual

then disrobed in accordance with tradition

Rabbit slaughter naked in the dim light

white fur stained red   pale skin streaked red

red pools on the marble floors   I bathe in red

Did I mention that I am of the noble class

You probably have noticed this already

Once I was beautiful but now   my face

my hands   my hair

Have you ever seen so much red

You see my father is ill   his heart is weak

I bring him tea   he does not drink

I mash ripe figs with a spoon

and press the thick paste to his lips

with the same spoon I gouge out

rabbit eyes and tell him   Father they are all blind now

I show him the spoon   their eyes   my hands

He nods his head beneath its heavy crown

MARY-KIM ARNOLD

My father's bed is the altar where we gather

all the blind rabbits and me

We know the armies are advancing

We can hear them sharpening steel

When they reach us   I will throw myself naked

across the body of my dead father

and they will see us   and they will know

from what nobility

                    we have descended

Reciprocal Identities

by Andrea Caswell

I admit a degree of relief that my youngest daughter is so different from me. My bookshelves are lined with novels and two editions of *The Norton Anthology of English Literature*, while hers contain *Measurement and Analysis of Random Data* and *Advanced Mechanics of Materials*. Ariane's favorite subject in college was thermodynamics; I swooned over French poetry. The flashcards of my life spell out obscure vocabulary words; hers show intricate formulas for *reciprocal identities* and *total arc length*. This divergence tells me that she went far beyond what I was capable of teaching her. It means that she became her own person.

    She's also different from her older sister, who was an American history buff by age nine. Ariane did not enjoy history. She didn't like memorizing names and dates, and wasn't sure what to do with all of that information afterwards. Learning foreign languages felt equally dull to her, not immediate somehow. What excited her most were math and science. I'll never forget one afternoon during her sophomore year of high school, when I asked, routinely, "How was your day?"

"The most amazing thing happened in geometry," she said. She was still a bit dazed, her limbic system buzzing. "I was sitting in class and then all of a sudden, I completely understood a cone."

She was on a steady path towards engineering. Her school offered CADD, or Computer-Aided Design and Drafting, which is used "to design and draft objects and materials using specialized software that visualizes designs as modular 3D computer models," according to the syllabus. Her teacher, Mr. Vatan, was an experienced civil engineer whose classroom was set up like a laboratory. Ariane created a map of the school for parents to use on Back-to-School Night. She remodeled a kitchen virtually using an advanced program called AutoCAD, down to the utensil organizers in drawers. She studied with Mr. Vatan all four years, eventually becoming his Teaching Assistant.

Junior year she signed up for "Introduction to Engineering." She was the only girl in a class of fifteen boys. Though she found the gender imbalance annoying, she loved the projects: making scale model houses out of foamboard, and testing temperatures in the various rooms using sensors; building an underwater vehicle with a PVC tube, installing motors for propulsion and steering, then taking it to a local pond for a trial run. They had competitions to see who could build the sturdiest structure with only paper and tape. She'd also been working on independent projects at home with the help of my dad, an aerospace engineer.

Ariane and her grandfather had started to speak the same language, about things like *servos* and *imaginary numbers*, though their conversations were limited to phone calls, since we lived in Boston and he in Oregon. When she was a junior, he sent her a box containing a circuit board and wires, a solid metal ball, and a mechanical teeter-totter (about eight inches wide) with a motor. Her job was to construct the device, then program the circuit board so the teeter-totter would roll the ball back and forth, without letting the ball fall off either end. It took her many months, with tiny parts laid out on the desk in her room, but she completed it.

By then we had started to visit colleges. We drove all day to Rensselaer Polytechnic Institute and toured the campus in the rain. The RPI student body was 70% male. On a trip to Pasadena, we visited the California Institute of Technology, with its red-tiled roofs and groves of orange trees. After the gauntlet of SAT subject tests and applications, she chose the School of Engineering at Roger Williams University in Bristol, Rhode Island. Following her high school graduation in 2013, we attended an orientation for incoming engineering students at RWU. As we filed into a light-filled auditorium, I was surprised to see that she was one of only several girls at the event. I remember thinking, somewhat backwardly, *Can't women be anything now?* While I wondered at the absence of female students, my daughter had expected it, and was happy to see even a few others in her midst.

Ariane chose mechanical engineering because, in her words, "I love physics."

Freshman year, she joined the campus chapter of the Society for Women Engineers (SWE). SWE's mission is to help women achieve their full potential in the industry, and to help them make an impact on the future. Ariane signed up because she wanted to meet other young women with similar goals, and to network with female professionals in the field.

Sometimes her SWE chapter organized STEM events for local Girl Scout troops. With girls as young as Brownies (ages 8-10), they made kaleidoscopes, raced pencils, assembled brush bots (small battery-operated vacuums), and constructed marshmallow catapults. Ariane's favorite event was an electrical engineering workshop; the goal was to light an LED bulb using only a lemon, a penny, and some nails. About halfway through the day, her group's bulb still wouldn't light up. She and her partner had to problem-solve on the spot. Was it the lemon? The bulb? The nails? Through trial and error, they figured out that the penny was at fault. The experiment's initial difficulties showed the girls in the workshop what engineering is all about: using mathematics and the natural laws of science to analyze, design, develop and devise improvements that benefit humanity.

Despite the supportive work of SWE, Ariane encountered painful setbacks her sophomore year. The first was Chemistry I, which she hadn't taken in high school and didn't understand, and now she was competing against students who'd aced AP Chem. She juggled chemistry with her other requirements, including statistics, a physics class with a lab, and a liberal arts requirement in literature and philosophy. Even more difficult was Calculus II, a core course for engineering majors. Students were allowed two attempts to pass; if they failed it twice, they were dismissed from the program. She failed the course the first time she took it.

The following semester, she again struggled with Calc II, and dropped the class when she learned she wouldn't pass. Though she received a 'W' on her transcript, the withdrawal would avoid a second fail, the strike that would end her quest to become an engineer. She received approval to take the course at a different college over the summer, since her school wouldn't be offering it then.

Bristol is a seaside town on Rhode Island's Narragansett Bay, about a hundred miles south of where my husband and I live. Ariane moved in with a family there, then drove nearly an hour each way to a class in Kingston three times a week. Though we were just a car-ride away in Massachusetts, I felt useless and afraid. What could I do to help her? What would happen to her—her future, her spirit—if she didn't pass this time? In two prior attempts at Calc II, she'd attended every extra help session offered by her teachers. She made appointments to speak with them during office hours, to review the problems she didn't understand. She'd completed test corrections whenever given the chance. Maybe she simply couldn't do differential equations, or handle *improper integrals* and *infinite series*. And who could blame her? Whatever those things were, they sounded impossible.

She got a 72 on the first test. The minimum passing grade was 70. On the second test, a 74.

I began to fear, as Ariane struggled, that the rhetoric I'd sold my daughters their entire lives might in fact be a sham. *Reach for the stars. You can achieve anything you set your mind to. Dream big.* These were refrigerator-magnet slogans, not preparation for their futures. We rarely tell our children how tough it will be, or that life is rock-hard and offers no guarantees. Ariane had a dream and she'd been working to achieve it for years. Yet here she was, on the verge of failing out of engineering school. I was heartbroken for her.

Though I tried to avoid it, my mind went to all the dark places when I imagined my daughter's bright future derailed. I worried it would break her, this terrible blow. It felt inherently unfair, though of course life is not fair, but she'd made so many sacrifices. Maybe she would lose faith in me too. I was the one who had pushed what now felt like irresponsible notions about dreams.

Whenever we talked on the phone that summer, I tried not to ask obsessive questions about the class. One Saturday she had plans to go to the beach with her friends—it was a glorious summer in Rhode Island, after all—and I thought, *Shouldn't she be studying?* I walked a fine line between being supportive and not increasing the pressure on her. If that's how terrifying it felt to me, what must it have been like for her?

I recently talked with her about those six weeks, and whether she allowed herself to think about failure. "I was always concerned about it," she said. "Every test score, every homework problem I didn't understand, every question I was afraid to ask, I would think

'Is this what's gonna end it all?' But that's why I had to suck up my pride and keep going to the professor for help."

When she wasn't sweating bullets over homework and tests, or enjoying a well-deserved moment outdoors, she worked for her thermodynamics teacher in a lab at Roger Williams. Her job was to assemble base robots and kits for the mechatronics class she would take senior year, if she could make it past Calc II. Mechatronics (a portmanteau of *mechanics* and *electronics*) is the "synergistic combination" of mechanical, electrical and software engineering. The teacher gave her a sample robot to copy. She made seven completed bases, and created kits of resistors, spare robot parts, wiring, tools, and test blocks. The robots would be programmed by students in the fall to perform autonomous tasks, such as navigating a maze and sorting balls of different colors.

In Calculus II she solved parametric equations and located polar coordinates. She defined improper integrals and found the properties of an infinite series. She scored 93 points on the final, and earned a B in the class. We treated her accomplishment like a birthday. We ate a cake with *Congratulations, Ariane* written in frosting on the top.

My dad recently rearranged some shelves in his workshop. All these years he'd saved his hardbound textbooks from engineering school, and he sent them to Ariane after she graduated last May. While visiting us for a weekend, she called him to discuss the books, which contained the same equations she'd learned in engineering school sixty years after he did. The laws of thermodynamics haven't changed. He must have told her about a few projects he's working on: a robot the size of a quarter, and a clock that can sense when people are in the room. I don't know exactly what he said to her, but she asked, "Is it in a different layer? If it's a hidden line, why would it show up?" She became thoughtful. "My solution would be to do a new layer, then draw the line and change the line type to a dash line instead of a hidden one."

I have no idea what any of that means, but I couldn't be happier for her.

Northern Goshawk
by Michael Hardin

Driving to a swim meet
we're watched by a goshawk
perched on the side of I-80
clutching its prey.

My son is nervous—
he does not notice the crow
mangled among the talons—
he fears disqualification.

By late December
when the trees are bare
the goshawks appear.

My son came in second,
swam a personal best.
The crow's my memory.

Eastern Screech Owl
by Michael Hardin

Outside my daughter's window—
she's eight—a screech owl
in a pilfered nest in the hollow
of a horse chestnut tree.

The squirrel squawks, glaring
first at me, then the owl
in her gray phase. She looks
like silver maple bark.

Beneath the trunk, a circle
of pellets, my daughter and I
the field mouse fur dissect.

By December the owl has flown,
the storm windows are closed,
down blankets my daughter.

Butter

by Joy Cooke

Long ago, when I was a child, when my grandmother was a good deal younger than I am now, I loved watching her make butter.

The uncles, young then and tanned and strong from daily hard work, milked the cows at dawn and dusk, sitting on their milking stools in their overalls, teasing us as we watched, their calloused hands expertly pumping the soft udders, propelling the milk into the stainless steel buckets until it foamed and frothed to the rim. The feral cats appeared, hoping, and the calves, penned nearby, waited bleating for their share.

The uncles carried the steaming, frothy buckets across the yard and up the porch steps into the kitchen. Coming through the door, the milk entered my grandmother's domain. They handed it over, as if an offering, and turned away to other tasks.

My grandmother handled the milk with reverence. She strained it through a fine cloth, then poured it into large pans and set it to rest, covered with another cloth, for a day. Set it to rest so the cream could rise – would rise. And it did. Mysteriously and magically, on the surface of the milk gathered a thick layer of yellow custardy cream, clumpy with rich butterfat – cream that must be spooned, not poured.

****

 She knows when it is ready. Carefully she skims the cream from the milk. The milk will be chilled, to be drunk up by thirsty uncles. The cream goes into a large bowl, to be made into butter. Sitting, it has taken up a natural tangy culture that is present in this place.

 She prepares the churn. The churn is a heavy earthenware crock, about 18 inches tall, with wooden handles, and a thick lid with a chip out of one side. A wooden dowel comes out through a hole in the center of the lid. To the bottom of this is affixed a cross made of two pieces of wood, to form the dasher. She washes the churn gently with warm water and soft soap.

 She waits for the quiet part of the day. After the midday meal and the dishes, when the cook stove has been allowed to cool down and the uncles have gone back to the work of the outdoors, when nothing is likely to disturb her, she sets the clean churn on a spread of newspaper in the middle of the floor. She sets her ladder-back chair beside it. I may watch, but I must be very quiet, and stay out of the way, an acolyte observing the priestess.

 She sits, in her worn apron, purses her lips a little, and begins to pump the dasher up and down, up and down. The sound is a rhythmic *kerplunk kerplunk kerplunk* as the cross on the dasher strikes the cream, stirring and disordering the globules with each strike, sloshing them against each other and the sides of the churn. My grandmother's bun begins to work loose, a strand of hair falling along her cheek, and she shines with a fine layer of sweat across her face. She pumps with concentration. She listens. She pauses. If it's a very warm day, she adds a little ice water to the churn. Pumps some more.

 Then, the pumping slows. She listens. A few more pumps, then she gives me a bare smile. "The butter's come," she says. She lifts the lid, raises the dasher. I am allowed to come off my chair and look. The dasher is covered with clumps and flecks of golden glistening butter.

Now she gets the large bowl. She reaches into the churn and lifts out handfuls of dripping, slippery butter, gathering the clumps into bigger clumps with her fingers. What's left in the churn is buttermilk, flecked with yellow bits of butter. It will be chilled and drunk up by thirsty uncles.

Now the butter must be washed. I stand on a stool at the sink and watch. She pushes cold water through the butter again and again with a wooden paddle until all the milk solids are removed, and the water runs clear, and the butter is pure butterfat. Then she will salt it lightly, form it into one pound loaves with her hands and wrap it in special paper, and it will be chilled. Some will be frozen, some she might sell. But this pound will be devoured on hot biscuits by hungry uncles and grandchildren, who don't know they will never taste anything like it again in their lives.

****

Now, I am older than my grandmother was then. Her churn sits in my house by the fireplace. The pole of the dasher is nearly worn through from years of scraping against the lid as it went up and down. In my house, it's a decorative, primitive piece. If I take the lid off, I can still smell the tang of the cream.

I look at it, and know what it has done, how hard it was worked, how hard they all worked. I look at it, and know that no one, after me, will carry that visceral memory of the ritual of butter making. No matter how many times I describe what I watched, they will not know it. I look at the churn and see its future – perhaps as a curiosity in a collectibles shop or antique emporium, valued as an object without a history, without a story, simply a quaint artifact from another time.

Prologue to a Stutter
by Kerri Sonnenberg

his first language is himself

the translation is running

to catch up

what you hear

is the running

*

so near
    his mouth—
a tiny moth

lands on his cheek   (the boy)

(he's four)   before I can even mention it

my pause

at the sight that may become a panic

spins itself off   onto the door the lock

disappears into the keyhole

Forward, Thinking

by Kerri Sonnenberg

I am counting on the silence of my debtors,
        as an architectural element of belief
        framing the errands of my day.
Lifting the window in the borrowed room,
I am inadvertently turning a red admiral into my prey.
I am flying back and forth
        a collection of mobilities
        entering countries with unearned grace.
Though at times I am not there to add my body to its autonomy.
Where I am habitually resident, my body can walk itself home
alone at night.
Where I am no longer resident but exist as a vague form of post,
a number on a single-unit
dwelling, a phantom limb
        feels its loss of rights.
Between two airplane windows, a representative
        of water makes a nervous trail
over Greenland which, consequently, is not the brailled white
        of the globes I believed.
The neighbors are creaking
where we are attached, our attachment
could also be the wind.
I don't know their names but they are masterful at not looking
in the direction of our screams,
return the balls that go over the fence.
Or is it the wind?
The wind that, given a name,

empties the shops of all their bread.
I was confident with a sharp edge held firmly in my hands until
they arrived with fire
and a total lack of hesitancy.
I am counting on this dream being merely an echo
of weather-related events
just as I am counting on a short visit from the neighbor
        kids who will touch everything in the house and then leave.
I am withholding water, as directed by the water authority.
More assertions begin "I feel" that at any other point in history.
I feel like I saw an aerial photo of the imprints of Neolithic
monuments, previously unknown,
revealed by unprecedented drought. But that's just me.
I have seen the recruitment, counted its young souls, filing out
from school too early.
It is in the category of arrivals, a sort of fume just outside
the window, but it smells like candy so the children are pleased.
I'll find out years from now if I should have worried.

Nathaniel

by Jim Mentink

*I*t was the year you turned fourteen and we found out Molly was allergic to olives. The year the snowmobile slid down the bank on its own accord, gliding across the frozen lake and falling through thin ice; the Polaris, the red one that Uncle Nick bought for you.

During that summer, two of the Finnegan kids beat you up. You cried but then made us laugh when you were grateful it hadn't been all the Finnegan kids, the seven of them lining up like a wedding reception striking you one at a time. The daughter, their eighth child, she wouldn't have beat you up. She and Molly used to play with dolls at the house and what was her name--Katrina--used to look at you like you were a rock star. You said so many mean things to her but she kept doting on you, joking that the two of you would be married.

It was the year the dog literally did eat your homework; the year Mom broke her wrist. I still remember Dad and Molly helping her into the car, that old station wagon, and rushing her to the hospital while I waited at home to let you know what happened. Do you remember what you said when I told you? "Is she going to live?" Fourteen years old and you were asking a silly question like that.

But you knew, didn't you?

I can't count the times your words have haunted me over the years. When I look at the clippings, when I remember the officers' somber faces, especially the pretty Hispanic cop who put her hand on our shoulders. As I think about the way you only stared blankly, as if you knew ahead of time the answer to your own question.

Then they took us to Grandpa's place and he and Grandma helped us finish school. When I brought up the crash with them, they always said things like "Oh, now, that's not pleasant to think about. Oughta be thinking about school or football." Smiling as they said it, as though they didn't acknowledge things.

They made us share a room. I remember it made you and me angry at first because they had two extra rooms crowded with their junk, but then we were glad to be together because the two of them were so distant from us, even when we were painfully close to them. And listening to Grandpa playing cards with those other guys, do you recall? Their voices traveling through the vents, giving each man a baritone quality whether or not he had one in reality. Grandma used to make us stay in our room because it was Grandpa's 'grown up' time, saying that even after we'd been in high school for a while.

But hearing their dirty jokes through the vents, and the coarse and profane terms, used to confuse us. You said once, I'm sure you remember, "Grandpa seems like such a sweet old man until his buddies show up." Even at that age, seventy or eighty, he was still trying to impress his friends. This bewildered and depressed us. We thought the need to impress others would never separate from us, but rather, follow us like a shadow on a long, sunny day.

You and I grew close at Grandma and Grandpa's and I even lived there an extra year while you finished high school. I did that so we could go to college together, something I've never told you, but I sense you always knew.

It wasn't because I liked working at the Dairy Bar. Most nineteen year olds were in college or working at the mall, but here I was working at the Dairy Bar with a bunch of underage girls, who giggled about stupid things and talked too quickly to the customers. In retrospect, I suppose I could be arrested for it, but I remember one night after work, going out to this one girl Carrie's car and smoking a cigarette with her. She thought I was this cool, rebel, uneducated older guy because I was pretty slick back then and working for that old pervert at the Dairy Bar. Pretty soon, we were in the back seat of her Plymouth having a winging of a time. It wasn't my first time; that was Kendra West, who told me you were her first, after. It kind of annoyed me that you'd beaten me to the punch and not mentioned it, but then I realized that it was just one more thing we shared.

When we went downstate to college, everything changed, didn't it? We drifted some and you wanted to stop talking about Mom, Dad and Molly. If I brought up the crash, you'd get a look of impatience in your eye. One time you looked like you wanted to throw a fist at my nose. I thought maybe it was your way of dealing with it, some kind of delayed denial thing. I was the tough leader during high school and you were trying to be the tough guy in college, that's how I interpreted it. I told myself that you'd open up if given the opportunity.

You and I shared a class in our sophomore year. One of the things we discussed was death and dying. The professor, the woman that wore those pleated skirts and had a permanent frown, asked if anyone had ever known someone close to them that had died. Do you remember?

I was painfully shy in large groups so I wasn't going to speak up but it surprised me that you didn't. She looked you in the eye because she knew. "Nathaniel," she said. "What about you? Anyone close to you ever die?" You looked like you were thinking about it and shook your head.

I almost died when you did that. It reminded me of Grandpa and Grandma and their 'now nows'. Wordsworth, that was the professor's name, the one with the pleated skirts.

We graduated from college during that awful spring when it snowed in late June. You had a degree in Communications and promptly took an assistant manager position at Luke Embry's Big and Tall Shop, a move that never made sense to me, especially with your voice. You thought I was crazy to head to the university upstate and get my M.A. in History. Looking back, I suppose you're right; the degree, just a piece of paper on the wall within the apartment of a bored mail carrier.

You married Kelly. Even though you and I had drifted quite a bit by that time, you asked me to be your best man. I was happy to do that. It was the first time I'd seen you really smiling, that afternoon that she gave her life to you. You looked like a rich man wearing that tuxedo, standing on the red velvet carpet waiting for her. And Kelly. God, was she beautiful. How a morose guy like you, who mumbled 'damn it all to hell' when his shoe became untied, won a girl like her, is beyond me. It makes no sense to bring this up now, but her cousin, the maid of honor that I was paired with, got pretty drunk with me later. We ended up in bed and dated for four months. You may have known that because she probably told Kelly.
Kelly.
Why did you hit her, Nathaniel? A kindergarten teacher with brilliant green eyes and perfect teeth, like she could do a toothpaste

ad and they wouldn't need to retouch the photos. They said you hit her once and caught her before she fell, only to hit her again as you held her. What was wrong with you? Who taught you that?

It filled me with rage when I pondered it and I decided you were an animal. I made a decision to pay a visit and talk some sense into you. I even filled my car up with gas to make the trip. But you know how I get about driving long distances, even four hours seems long sometimes. I fall asleep. I can't do that.

I thought about calling you and telling you off, but when I went to dial the phone I saw the bottles of Jim Beam lined up on my kitchen counter and my copy of Barely Legal under the phone directory and I decided that maybe it'd be hypocritical.

Kelly healed nicely but you never knew it because she left you right after that. She had been two months pregnant when you hit her and it had upset her so much, she tearfully aborted it, which distanced her from her father, the Presbyterian minister.

You were especially dark for the year or two after she left. I was so mad at you for hitting her, even after the time had passed, that when I married Bianca I didn't ask you to be my best man. I didn't even invite you, but you showed up, anyway. You forgave me, I forgave you and we got drunk. Really drunk.

So drunk that my new wife thought I was an idiot. There we were, you and I, smelling like we slept in a beer barrel, laughing like schoolgirls and laying on the floor of the reception hall. Bianca came in, telling me we needed to go because the flight was leaving at ten that night. She was right, but you told her to go without me because we were having plenty of fun without her. I was too drunk to care.

Thankfully, she forgave me under the condition that I never see you again. Which I didn't until now.

Your place was a mess, a garden of magazines and old newspapers. Pizza boxes were strewn across tables, ants and roaches outnumbered the dust bunnies. The place smelled like a cross between steamed rice, mustard and sweat.

I didn't want to stay long but the lawyer, your lawyer he said, wanted me to check to see if there was anything I wanted. Bianca waited in the car while I looked; she'd driven because I fall asleep during long drives--you know that.

I found nothing I needed or wanted in your apartment. You had a closetful of big and tall clothes despite your being a slight and wiry man. Your pillowcase looked like it hadn't seen the inside of a washing machine for a decade and when I went to open your refrigerator, the handle came off.

The last thing I did before I left your apartment was to walk into the living room where you had lain. There was a faint imprint of your body, the sweat I guess, on the carpeting. They said you'd taken seven of those pills, what were they? They told me four would kill a man so you must have been damn sure you were more than a man. At first, I thought that's an awful thing to say to the man's brother; but then I remembered how we weren't getting along, anyway, and I laughed.

I came to your place with nothing and I left with nothing. When I got back into the car, Bianca said you were nothing. I said nothing.

As we headed out of town and began the long trek home, I thought of something you'd said to me when we were at Grandpa's, sitting by the vent. You said, "How does someone get that bad?" I told you I didn't know. You said, "If I ever get that bad, I hope I don't have grandkids around to know about it."

Mission accomplished, Nathaniel. Good-night.

Appliances

by Meg Yardley

On Tuesday the latch knob hurtles off the toaster,
startles me, small silver bullet of the morning.
On Wednesday, pressing down the lever,
I flinch and take a half step back.
On Thursday, we can only use the right side.

The sunken toast in the left unit cools
and shrinks back to bread, flakes off
on the knife dipping down to draw it up.
On Friday, the "warm" setting
sears my store-brand slice to cinders.

The first foible was funny, our kitchen fable,
but soon we're fixed to new formations:
making the kids' breakfast one slice at a time,
leaning on the lever at arms' length,
wondering out loud whether these things

are even made to be repaired
or if we'll just keep living around them.

The Plain

by Ruth Lepson

after Brueghel's "The Peasant Wedding"
and William Carlos Williams' poem

Bowls and white tablecloth and plain brown walls.

Bonnet, cap or hat.

A placid young girl sits on the floor, tasting something.

No one's beautiful, some faces are barely formed.

Even the whitish dog with its long pointed nose is homespun.

A kindly one pours beer from a clay jug.

White caps and aprons add areas of brightness.

Plain black shoes, dark green leggings.

Bits of gold, red jackets, cool greens and yellow ochre.

They're drinking like babies.

The long wood table juts out at a diagonal.

RUTH LEPSON

The bride wears a special collar, her hands folded.

Her hair's long and flat.

She wears a red headband and sits in front of a green cloth.

A sword, a tie under the knee, bagpipes.

Brueghel's satisfaction in painting the surfaces.

A brown woven basket.

A plain wooden spoon in a young boy's hatband.

The food is plain, clabber perhaps.

One man looks hopeful—today some extra wine.

Someone's trying to get through the doorway with a platter of food and more drink.

It's tight back there.

A young girl stuffs food in her mouth.

A child is licking a finger with the last of the food.

Large areas of color and shape.

He made these paintings that have come down to us.

A peacock feather perhaps symbolic of rebirth.

The children look old and blameless.

Out the rear door, trees and white sky.

A plain life, and a day when a little more is given.

You see he loved to paint the hands, the wheat bales, the crossed
    sheaves.

Brueghel's interest in the backs of necks, the rounded faces.

William Carlos Williams,
Pediatrician, visitor to the homes of Polish mothers,
    Writes a plain poem about the painting,
        Just what pertains.

Parts of faces are blocked by other people.

What you might expect to be the center is not the center.

No one is looking at anything.

The people are crowded together
as they often are and every passage through life
a celebration.

Chisinau, 2017

by Flora Lindsay-Herrera

There are moments of stillness and moments of motion. The evening of my arrival in Chisinau, I take a slow walk down the frozen city streets, past a kitchenwares store, a bookshop, and a market with sausages and imported chocolates illuminated in the window. I reach as far as an Orthodox churchyard, but it is dark and the sidewalk are black ice, so I double back to the hotel. Every first night in a new place starts like this: with a walk and a half breath.

I'd come to Moldova for work, but driven by a yearning for stillness. Back home, too much speed had led to a skiing accident and knee surgery, and during my recuperation I missed public hearings on a major development project that turned my home's views of trees and blue sky to concrete. All the knee aches, the heartache, the loss of control meant I spent afternoons in the office meditation room, sitting on the floor with shuddering sobs.

So, Chisinau in January, for a five month assignment. I'd brought a camera here, and a watercolor set, but the gray of mid-winter Chisinau managed to not even be charismatically ugly enough for art. Before my departure I had hunted for writings on Moldova, and found Anne Applebaum: "Kishinev had always lain on the edges of empire….however, none of Kishinev's rulers had ever thought enough of the city to make it beautiful," she wrote, in the early 1990's.

The daylight walks in my first weeks bear out her assessment: a mixture of 19th century houses that survived WWII bombing, an enormous Soviet circus, and phone stores blaring EDM. Incrementally, more cracks in the Parisian-wide sidewalks emerge as the ice dripped away in early March. Overhead, tramlines spark, and the one microbus I dare take is so crammed that a stranger offers to hold my handbag on her lap.

There are other small wonders, though. Like watching grandmothers sprint across glaciated paths to catch the tram – remember, my co-worker Diana says, they've had a lifetime of practice. Wonders, and joys – the wine, free wifi in the parks, my co-workers' easy trilingualism.

Wonders: creamed soups, chicken soups, borscht. And bafflement, the first time I try to find soup in the grocery store. Oh no, says my Romanian teacher, appalled at the notion. Soup isn't sold at the grocery store. Soup is for homes and restaurants. The store is for a dozen types of corn meal, plump pomegranates and persimmons, rows of milks and yogurts (never exactly the same brands from day to day), and labels in both Cyrillic and Latin scripts that keep me guessing and that turn buying packaged spices into a thirty minute jigsaw of photos, transliteration, and translation.

Chisinau, Moldova: the Turkish Airlines flight map depicts this former Soviet breadbasket as an unnamed body of water. Flights to Chisinau leave in the bus station-esque part of regional airports, on the ground floors so the shuttle buses can better transport passengers to tiny prop planes. In Bucharest, the gates are behind the food court; in Kiev, at the farthest reach of the departures corridor. In

Ataturk, Istanbul, the lower level is chaos, and the chances are high of missing the boarding call and ending up on a turboprop bound for Skopje or Pristina instead.

When Molotov and Ribbentrop laid down the faultlines of the wartime east, Moldova (then part of Bessarabia) came within the Soviet sphere of influence. German occupation, then Soviet reclamation, in 1945. Deportations, resettlement, regifting of the Black Sea port to Ukraine; independence in 1991; a brief civil war and Russian-established foothold in the breakaway region of Transnistria; EU aspirations; Russian recriminations. A week after the United States' 2016 elections - three months before my arrival - a pro-Russia candidate won Moldova's presidency in a run-off election against the pro-E.U. education minister. All 2017 he routinely squares off against a pro-EU parliament that toys with the prospect of impeaching him.

The currents of empires eddy through these borderlands. At a folk dance festival, there are Roma dances, Ukrainian ones, Russian, Gaugaz, Romanian ones, and, in a moment of decontextualized dislocation, an Israeli settler dance. The kids working my kebab shop always speak to me in English, but the mobile phone hires mostly stick to Romanian. I am in a fashion show, and the makeup girls speak Romanian, but the hairstylists – like most of the industry folks I encounter – use Russian. At a soccer game, the concessions guy insists on serving us piwo instead of birre, but when the Tiraspol team wins the match, four of their players whip out a Brazilian flag. My colleague's Moldovan mother communicates with her Colombian son-in-law and me in a mixture of Italian, Romanian, and pantomime. I am introduced to two members of the Alliance Francaise, one of whom immediately says something snarky in French about the untrustworthiness of US government employees. The other, as an afterthought, asks me a few minutes later if I speak French. *Oui, je comprend.*

Moldova is empty space on the Turkish Airlines map, but in defiance of cartography my Dominican mother landed here in the 1970s, as part of a peace tour. She remembers a priest celebrating Mass in an unmarked house out in the countryside, a necessity in an era of Soviet anti-religious campaigns. He'd had his back to the congregation and spoke in Latin, still in the old ways, as if Vatican II hadn't happened. Come Eastertime, my visiting boyfriend and I attend part of an Orthodox Easter service in a small parish church. Our host is a university student who has come home from Chisinau to help at her parents' guesthouse. It is midnight, so she walks us by smartphone flashlight through the darkened village of Lalova to the chapel. Parishioners take shifts standing and sitting through the hours-long service, against the susurration of priest and congregation in a cyclical call and response: *hristos a înviat, adevârat a înviat!*.... An old woman sits in the darkened vestibule to rest awhile, her kerchief illuminated in the candlelight.

There are moments of motion and moments of stillness. A terrible April snowstorm hits Chisinau a week after Easter and we are not sure which moment this is. Leaf-laden branches have fallen in the heavy unyielding snow, trees have fallen, power lines have fallen, but we have a flight to Bucharest. I make us a breakfast of muesli with Greek yogurt and pomegranate seeds while we debate the options. The power goes out. In an unfamiliar country, the parameters are unknown. What kind of taxis, what kind of ground crews, what sort of mettle. My boyfriend wants to stay in and snuggle under the covers. I want to try for the airport. I had come here for stillness, but I find myself moving, always moving – I am pathological, maybe, or intrepid, or foolhardy. . . .

Because, in an autocratic decision I bet on mettle. We take an SUV that inches down the airport road past lines of hitchhikers. The airport has power, hot sausages, and white wine. Six hours later, a twin prop plane with three flights' worth of passengers takes off with a shudder. When I return to Chisinau alone after four days, the snow is gone and broken trees splay everywhere.

A week after the snowstorm, I find myself with coworkers in a hot air balloon basket floating over the farmlands and valley of Orhei. Despite the windy day, the basket is blessedly still - of course it is, we laughingly realize - we are moving at the speed of the wind. Stillness in motion, until the basket bounces to a skidding halt in a fallow field and we all come tumbling out.

That same weekend I befriend two Moldovan actors at a May Day wine festival. One of them is a tennis-loving playboy and the other is producing Hamlet with life inmates in a maximum security prison in the north of Moldova. He invites me to the performance. The prison is near the banks of the Raut, across the river from Transnistria. Thirty three percent of Moldova's inmates face sentences of more than ten years, and the 103 inmates here are in for life. The actors face a minimum of 25 years before the dubious and elusive possibility of parole.

The production takes place in the prison yard, with the sun going down behind the set and the other inmates watching from cells that wall the yard in. It is cold, and a motley collection of jackets appear, a generous loan from our captive hosts to warm the crowd. A gull flaps above the stage. Denmark is a prison, this jail is a prison, but the actors do what they can to keep their spirits in motion. The actor who plays Hamlet has spent a decade in prison, uncertain decades to go, and will marry his girlfriend of three years soon. You should write about that, the tennis player tells me.

I am doing a lot of writing, mostly thinking about motion as choice, as chance, as necessity. A dear friend tells me – you are running away. My boyfriend isn't sure why I won't come home. But cities all smell the same in the summer, and everywhere is home. Old women sell cherries on the street corner and little boys chase pigeons on the Cathedral plaza. Chisinau has not disappointed me, yet. But put otherwise, the weight of reality is not yet a burden in this place.

With its seeds swaddled in pith and saran wrap, the other half of my snowstorm pomegranate (an out-of-season gift from the central market) lasts a month. In this time, the mayor of Chisinau is arrested on suspicion of corruption, the Liberal party withdraws from the ruling coalition in protest, and the lilacs and peonies bloom. The Hamlet producer and I take a lemonade together on a sunny May afternoon so I can return a jacket that his girlfriend forgot at my house. We talk about the world, at once as big and as small as two strangers who met for the first time as old friends. Life, he says, is a provocation.

In a future present, when the world has shrunk back down to the routine of work home gym and back again, his words are a remembrance of the unscripted promise of the world. In the moment, they are a consolation. I am going back to Washington in a week, and maybe everything will be ok. Not all change is running away. Maybe it can be the long way home.

Even for my five month stay though, there is paperwork. To get my residency visa, and then to extend it, takes at least ten trips to the Bureau of Migration. Some of these trips are more successful than others, but my Romanian gets stronger too, and finally I get the staff to break from script and crack a smile. On my final walk to the Migration Bureau I look up and take pictures of facades that are crumbling but elegant. I earn permission to stay, a weekend and five business hours before my flight home. In Romanian, the verb to thank is non-transitive, *a multumi*. I thank, in an act of boundless gratitude.

The weekend before my flight home, I meet with friends for an open air opera. We picnic on the banks of the river Raut: four Americans, a Frenchwoman and her Anglo-Moldovan husband, and their Afghan-Gaugazian friend. The Frenchwoman asks us Americans if we've ever seen bears in America and is delighted when we say yes. She says she prefers places where nothing happens - and yet, here there is so much happening that maybe she does not see? Molecules still move here and chance is the same. We drink Fetească Neagră and watch sheep across the stream. The axes of the world are shifting, there is stillness in the motion, and thus provoked, we watch the goats ascend the cliff face and the birds fly by. We exhale.

It is a different kind of love, when you see someone day in, day out.

Thus provoked, how to apprehend the world and stay still enough to feel its wonders?

The world, as infinity, as bounded as two recent strangers who share its wonders. And in a future now.

A co-worker asked me what I learned. How to apprehend the world. Affirmation. New questions, what to do with partner who brought me the pomegranate, who waits for me in what will never be my only home.

Ni Pena Ni Miedo
by David Green

Some people must wonder why we want bones.
I want them so much! I want them so much!
        --Violeta Berrios in *"Nostalgia for the Light"*

In Chacabuco in the open air,
the half-buried remains
of *Pampinos*, the nitrate men,
like geological layers swept by wind.

A land permeated with salt,
no insects, no animals, no birds.
Mummified remnants, blankets, and shoes.

Not pebbles washed up by the sea.
Not cairns to mark the way. Not stones thrown.
The fragments too white, too smooth,
too like thighbone, or arm.

A mother tries to find her son
by touch. It is her hand, not her voice
that calls out to him. The memory
in her fingers plays like
a broken accordion.

There is no song here,
only the incessant wind.

DAVID GREEN

An abandoned whitewashed
house, where the names on the walls
crumble, letters missing –
Rene Olivares, E… Pat… lli, Federico… Q… C
What is left, the cloudless
irrevocable descent of the sun.

A hand shovel
and endless salt.

It is said that in the desert you become
more silent than the silence around you,
then suddenly hear silence speak --

here, syllables of human petroglyphs.

Each word is washed, each bone.
*Tomó Jesús el pan, y bendijo, y lo partió, y dió á sus discípulos,
y dijo: Tomad, comed, esto es mi cuerpo.*

The *duelo* is wind.
The *duelo* is salty dirt.
The *duelo* is a body broken.

Night arrives like a door kicked in
wind full of bones and hair.
Nowhere to run.

                    Awake in the dark
stars light up, tens by hundreds
by thousands. The past beyond the past,
light of a billion bodies arriving.

To feel their gravitational pull,
secrets that have been travelling forever.
A light rain of names begins to fall.

Baking for the Masses

by Zachary Spence

"Bakers, welcome back to another round of *Baking for the Masses!*" The host beamed at the contestants, gaze sliding just above the level of the TV camera trained her way. "As you know, each week we prepare a special ingredient for you, which must star in a recipe of your choosing. Our judges will sample your bakes, and one baker will be eliminated from the competition. Naturally, the loser will be fed to the Masses.

"Tonight's key ingredient is olive oil. You'll find a bottle of it on your benches. Use as little or as much as you like, but we want you to create a satisfying dessert that incorporates the key ingredient. You have two hours. Now... bake for the Masses!"

The three remaining contestants leapt to action: there was Germaine, who'd lived in Bledlow all her life, had three daughters of 5, 6, and 8, and worked part-time at the library; Steven, a newlywed who baked as stress relief from his volunteer firefighter role; and Penelope, a recent law school graduate who wore chunky sweaters and chunky bracelets and kept her red hair in a ponytail.

Each of the three had their own workbench crowded with glass bowls, whisks, measuring cups, spoons, and ball jars full of flour and sugar. The olive oil shimmered darkly at the head of their tables. The workbenches sat twenty feet apart within a shared tent, the ceiling a heavy, drooping white and the walls clear plastic. Early on, the competitors had chatted with each other across the room, back when there had been more than a dozen of them. Now that their numbers had dwindled to three, they didn't speak much.

Germaine grabbed a bottle of white wine and poured some into a bowl. She tossed in a handful of anise seeds and set her timer for one hour. She wouldn't lose this competition—she couldn't. She needed to show her daughters that she could win. That if ever they were forced to compete on *Baking for the Masses*, they could survive.

That was her only option left. Her goal, now that the original plan to poison the Masses had proven impossible.

It was the host who had shattered that dream during the perfunctory orientation. The contestants had gathered in the tent, twitching at every distant shriek from the pit outside. The Masses hadn't been fed human flesh—the only thing that really calmed them—in nearly a year.

"The Masses eat everything. Anything. It can be burnt, it can be sour, it can be made by my sister—just kidding!—heck, they'll eat the tin the pie comes in and wash it down with bleach. You really can't do wrong by them." Then the host, slender in a silver suit, had laughed. "But of course you can do wrong by us."

So now Germaine's only option, her only Plan B, was to win. To get back home to her daughters a champion.

To get back home to her daughters at all.

Penelope's plan never involved the Masses. She was smarter than that. At her workbench, she rolled up the sleeves of her favorite orange paisley sweater—one she never would've worn while baking if she wasn't on the show—and filled a bowl with cashews, walnuts, pumpkin seeds, and golden raisins. She poured in maple syrup and drizzled olive oil over the top, then tossed it all together and laid it out in a pan.

Each bench came equipped with an oven. As she knelt down to fiddle with the settings on it, something moved out of the corner of her eye. Her head jerked in the direction of the tent wall. A perpetual mist, thickening into rain, obscured the finer details beyond the transparent plastic. The sloping green field blurred into a smudge of trees in the distance. Between here and there a mottled lump loped across her view. There were appendages, white and black and purple. Then the thing launched itself out of sight, at a speed too fast to follow. Beyond the tent walls erupted the panicked bleating of a sheep, then silence.

Masses, Penelope thought. She reached into the oven and used her mitted hand to shake the tray of granola. Impatient monsters, the lot of them. That's why she didn't bother with them. Instead, she focused on the other contestants. Figured out what they were making, then made sure they were just barely short an ingredient. It would be too obvious to hide a whole bag of desiccated coconut, but if someone needed a cup and she took all but a half-cup, well then, they needed to change their plans last minute or else risk the judges saying they couldn't taste one of their flavors.

Speaking of. She looked back at the bench behind her. Arranged in front of him Steven had a pyramid of eggs, a bag of shelled pistachios, and a vanilla bean split open like a body mid-autopsy. He was using what looked like a dental pick to scrape out the seeds. At his elbow were the olive oil bottle and the standard jars of flour and sugar. Nothing exotic at all, certainly nothing the staff would be short-handed on.

Penelope made a show of fumbling her jar of salt. An avalanche of it tumbled down her chest and ended up in her apron pocket. She dumped blueberries and sugar in a pan, and cream and vanilla in her ice cream maker, before she hurried over to Steven's bench. As her shadow fell into his mixing bowl, his head snapped back. His eyes were deep set and haunted.

"Steven, have you more eggs?" she asked quickly. She gestured behind her at her sizzling pan, her flashing oven light, her ice cream maker with its open lid. "I'm short, please tell me you've more!"

"Yes, hold on, hold on—" Steven snapped to attention, looked everywhere along his bench.

"You need all those?" she asked, moving aside his sugar jar to reveal his pyramid of brown eggs.

"Yes—the fridge—" He made a break for the refrigerator at the back of the room. He came back with four eggs clutched in one massive palm, his fingers long and unsettling, cradling the delicate shells.

Penelope thanked him, slid them into her apron, returned to her bench.

Steven felt sweat fill the creases of his forehead. *Will be me next,* he thought, *me next.*

Must focus. Or me next.

His pals at the firehouse had reassured him when they heard he'd been chosen to participate. "You'll kill it," they'd told him, an ominous prediction. To date he hadn't killed any of them, and there was certainly far more than one of "it." Would that he could kill them! Would that he had his fireman's axe! But District Chief Lou, who everyone said had personal experience with the Masses, went all glass-eyed at the suggestion that they could be killed with an axe. *Son I'll put it this way; they don't react the way you think they will.*

Stop thinking about them! Steven beat sugar and butter together. He cracked eggs one-handed into his mixer as it whirred. A thousand times, he'd made this cake—perhaps more. He made twenty of them for the Firefighter's Fundraiser every year, and he made them for his Monday night shifts every week, and he made them for his wife to bring to the elementary school where she worked.

That was one advantage he had—he wouldn't need to stop and taste and adjust like the other two would. He had faith in himself, in this recipe. He poured olive oil into the mixer in a slow stream. It glittered, dark drops of it spattering the sides of the bowl. He winced, looked away. No, he certainly wouldn't be taste-testing this.

"Bakers, your time is *up!*" shouted the host in the silver suit. She beamed at the three bakers, who looked as exhausted and floured as they did every night. The two judges stood on either side of her, one an elderly Asian man with papery lips and bottle cap glasses, the other a young woman in a blood red dress. "Let's start with you, Germaine; please bring your dessert to the front."

Germaine presented her ciambelline al vino to the judges, who bit into the ring-shaped cookies with their best poker faces.

"Good," said Peter Zhelan, who had four high-end restaurants in Hong Kong and a growing chain of "authentic Chinese food for the European palate" places across England and France. "I can taste anise seed. Nice crunch to it."

The woman in red, August Montgomery, was the executive head chef for the hotel at which foreign dignitaries stayed when they visited Washington D.C. She waved her hands when she spoke, two fingers pinching a ciambelline moon. "It's so wonderfully subtle. I'm picking up the wine, I'm picking up the fruitiness from the olive oil. Well done, Germaine."

Penelope brought up her dessert next. "It's blueberry ice cream with homemade granola."

The judges tried each element separately, then together.

"Maple," said Peter. "You baked the granola with maple and olive oil? It's very clever."

"A fun combination," August called it. "Together or sep—"

From overhead came a screech, sharp and prolonged but only just loud enough to interrupt her, as if a pointed rebuke of her feedback. The sound tapered off into an almost-human groan. Long indentations appeared in the ceiling of the tent, accompanied by the squeal of nails running down the heavy plastic. Peter's eyes drifted upwards.

The noise stopped.

"Together or separately," finished August with a smile. She looked at the sweating man in the back of the room. "Steven?"

He brought up his olive oil cake, topped with pistachios and a lemon-sugar glaze, then wordlessly stepped back to await judgment.

Peter Zhelan cut the cake. Both judges murmured about how well the bake looked inside. They took bites.

Immediately both of them blanched. Steven felt a cold fear break out in his stomach.

"What—what's—?"

"Steven, did you put salt in this?" asked Peter.

"Quarter teaspoon."

"Not a chance," August said. She shook her head roughly. "Tastes like you added a few *table*spoons. It's inedible."

"What? But I didn't—I didn't—"

Behind him, Penelope watched stone-faced. She felt neither remorse nor joy. She felt gratitude towards her grandpa who had shown her sleight-of-hand tricks as a child. She felt relief that she would live to see the next round. That she would live.

Two colossal men entered the tent and grabbed Steven around the biceps, near-lifting him off the ground. He struggled, shouted for mercy—"There's been some mistake! Please, please! I've made it a thousand times!"—but even the volunteer firefighter could not break free of the guards' grasp. They dragged him outside, and a minute later, the remaining contestants heard a guttural scream, and when that stopped all of a sudden, they were left with only the horrible crunch of bones.

"Well, ladies," said the host with a grin, "congratulations on making it to the finals of *Baking for the Masses*! We'll see you back in the tent tomorrow night for the final round, when the special ingredient will be Steven flour. Make sure you get plenty of rest tonight, and remember to lock your doors and windows to keep out the Masses—good night!"

Contributors

V. N. Alexander is a literary fiction novelist (*Smoking Hopes*, 1994; *Naked Singularity*, 2003; *Trixie*, 2010; and *Locus Amoenus*, 2015) published by The Permanent Press. She is also a philosopher of science working on creativity, evolutionary adaptation, and learning. She is a Rockefeller Foundation Bellagio Center alum, a former Public Scholar for the New York Council for the Humanities, and is currently at ITMO University in St. Petersburg, Russia on a Fulbright grant doing art/science research. Her science publications include *The Biologist's Mistress: Rethinking Self-Organization in Art, Literature and Nature*, 2011 and a contribution to *Fine Lines: Vladimir Nabokov's Scientific Art*, published by Yale University Press, which was one of *Nature*'s Top 20 Books of 2016.

Diannely Antigua is a Dominican American poet and educator, born and raised in Massachusetts. Her debut collection *Ugly Music* (YesYes Books, 2019) was the winner of the Pamet River Prize. She received her B.A. in English from the University of Massachusetts Lowell where she won the Jack Kerouac Creative Writing Scholarship and received her MFA at NYU where she was awarded a Global Research Initiative Fellowship to Florence, Italy. She is the recipient of additional fellowships from CantoMundo, Community of Writers, and the Fine Arts Work Center Summer Program. Her work has been nominated for both the Pushcart Prize and Best of the Net. Her poems can be found in *Washington Square Review, Bennington Review, The Adroit Journal, Cosmonauts Avenue, Sixth Finch*, and elsewhere. Her heart is in Brooklyn.

Mary-Kim Arnold is the author of *Litany for the Long Moment* (Essay Press, 2018) and *The Fish & The Dove* (Noemi Press, 2020). She teaches in the Nonfiction Writing Program at Brown University. "Legacy" is from Mary-Kim's new collection, *The Fish & The Dove*, published by Noemi Press in 2020.

Tanushree Baidya is a Kweli fellow, a graduate of the Yale Writers' Workshop and a member of the (GrubStreet supported) Boston Writers of Color group. Her work has appeared in *Creative Nonfiction, Kweli, Florida Review, 2040 Review, Grubwrites, London Journal of Fiction*, and elsewhere. She won an honorable mention in Tom Howard/John H. Reid Fiction & Essay Contest 2018. Born in India, Tanushree has lived in Boston since moving there from Bombay eight years ago. In her parallel life, she's an analyst with a degree in engineering and MBA in Finance. She can be found on Twitter (@tanushreebb) and Instagram (@tinksfloyd).

Amy Bernstein's short story "Lamp Repair" received honorable mention in *Glimmer Train* magazine in 2018, and was published in *The Forge* magazine in March of 2019. She was the recipient of 2017, and 2018 PEN America, Press Freedom Incentive Fund Grants. Her short stories, "Upon Leaving The Hospital," appeared in *Black Heart Magazine* and "Volunteer Garden," in *Cease Cows*. Her short story "Missing in Action" won the One City, One Story Competition at the Boston Book Festival in 2014. Her children's story, and math book, *Time Travel Math*, was published by Prufrock Press in 2010. She is a member of Grub Street Writers Workshop in Boston, and a PEN America Writing Professionals Member.

Andrea Caswell holds an MFA from the Bennington Writing Seminars, and is a fiction editor at *Cleaver Magazine*. Her work has been published by *River Teeth*, *The Normal School*, *Fifth Wednesday Journal*, *Atticus Review*, and others. In 2019 she was selected as a fiction participant for the Sewanee Writers' Conference. A native of Los Angeles, Andrea now teaches writing in Newburyport, Massachusetts.

Marisa P. Clark, a native of the Mississippi Gulf Coast and former resident of Atlanta, is a queer writer whose work has appeared in *Apalachee Review*, *Cream City Review*, *Ontario Review*, and *Sinister Wisdom*, among others. Her creative nonfiction was recognized among the Notable Essays in *Best American Essays, 2011*. She makes her home and living in New Mexico and also serves as a fiction reader for *New England Review*.

Joy Cooke lives in central Massachusetts in a constant state of wonder. She writes memoir, short fiction, and poetry, influenced by her southern heritage, her New England education, and the wonderful writers in her life.

Justin Danzy is a Chancellor's Graduate Fellow at Washington University in St. Louis, where he is completing his MFA. He was the 2019 Gregory Pardlo Fellow at the Frost Place Poetry Seminar and a finalist for the Knightville Poetry Contest. His poems have appeared or are forthcoming in *West Branch* and *Guesthouse* among other places. He is a member of Westside Missionary Baptist Church in St. Louis. Justin is from Southfield, Michigan.

Jose Hernandez Diaz is a 2017 NEA Poetry Fellow. He's from Southern California. His work appears in *The Acentos Review, Bat City Review, Cincinnati Review, Huizache, Iowa Review, The Nation, Poet Lore, The Progressive, Witness*, and in the *Best American Nonrequired Reading 2011*. His chapbook of prose poetry *The Fire Eater* is forthcoming with Texas Review Press in Spring 2020.

Franklin Einspruch is an artist and writer in Boston. Earlier this year he was the Fulbright/Q21-MuseumsQuartier Artist-in-Residence in Vienna.

E. Thomas Finan is the author of the short story collection *The Other Side*. His essays and fiction have been published in *The Atlantic, Prairie Schooner, Vol. 1 Brooklyn, The Millions*, and elsewhere. He teaches at Boston University.

Christina Marsden Gillis lives most of the year in Berkeley, California, where she administered the Center for the Humanities at the University of California, but having spent every summer of her adult life on an island in Maine, she considers herself an "island writer". She is the author of *Writing on Stone: Scenes from a Maine Island Life* (2008), and more recently (2017), *Where Edges Don't Hold*, a finalist for best book in Maine-themed non-fiction, an award offered by the Maine Writers and Publishers Association. Her work has appeared in journals as diverse as *House Beautiful, Island Journal, Hotel Amerika, Women's Studies, Raritan, Southwest Review*, and *Bellevue Literary Review*. Pieces appearing in the latter three were listed as "notable essays" in *Best American Essays*.

David Green is a clinician working in a community health center in Jamaica Plain, MA. He was raised in Venezuela. Previously published poems have appeared in the *Lyric Review* and the *Bellevue Literary Review*.

Mark Halpern has lived since 1993 in Tokyo, where he runs his own law firm and writes stories about foreigners in Japan. He was born in America, grew up mostly in Canada, and has spent substantial time in the UK and France. As for Japan, Mark has, like some of his stories' characters, found a way to be both an outsider and an insider.

Michael Hardin, originally from Los Angeles, now lives in rural Pennsylvania with his wife, two children, and two Pekingeses. He is the author of a poetry chapbook, *Born Again* (Moonstone Press 2019), and has had poems published in *Seneca Review, Connecticut Review, North American Review,*

Quarterly West, Gargoyle, Texas Review, Tampa Review, among others. He has recently finished his memoir, *Touched*.

Chris Hartman is a 1985 graduate of Hartwick College. He is the author of one book, *Advance Man: The Life and Times of Harry Hoagland*; editor of the novels *Sons of Granada*, by Carl Jeronimo, and *The Last Columnist*, by Tom Morgan, as well as several other books. He has also contributed numerous book reviews and features to the *Christian Science Monitor, Upstate Diary*, and other publications. He presented at the 2006 Business History Conference held at the University of Toronto's Munk Centre, has been an event producer at several Boston Book Festivals, and served for five years as Vice President of Bookbuilders of Boston.

Tanya Larkin teaches first year writing and poetry writing at Tufts University. She lives with her young son in Somerville, MA. She is the author of *My Scarlet Ways* (Saturnalia) and *Hothouse Orphan* (Convulsive Editions.) Her latest poems have appeared in *Sixth Finch, BOAAT*, and *The Critical Flame*.

Michael J. Leach is an academic, statistician and poet who enjoys combining science with art. He works in a multidisciplinary environment at the Monash University School of Rural Health. Michael's poems reside in *Cordite Poetry Review, Meniscus Literary Journal*, the *Medical Journal of Australia, The Mathematical Intelligencer, Plumwood Mountain, GRAVITON*, the *Antarctic Poetry Exhibition*, and elsewhere. His debut poetry collection – a science-themed chapbook – is forthcoming from Melbourne Poets Union. He lives in Bendigo, Australia.

Ruth Lepson is poet-in-residence at the New England Conservatory of Music and her most recent book is *Ask Anyone*, which comes with musical settings on her website, ruthlepson.com.

Flora Lindsay-Herrera is a librarian, but previously worked as project director for an international development consulting firm. She lives in Washington, D.C. and can be found online at vidauruguaya.tumblr.com.

Ron MacLean is author of the story collections *We Might as Well Light Something on Fire* and *Why the Long Face?*, and the novels *Headlong* and *Blue Winnetka Skies*. His fiction has appeared in *GQ, Narrative, Fiction International*, and elsewhere. MacLean is a recipient of the Frederick Exley Award for Short Fiction and a multiple Pushcart Prize nominee. He holds a Doctor of

Arts from the University at Albany, SUNY, and teaches at Grub Street in Boston.

Jennifer Markell's first poetry collection, *Samsara*, (Turning Point, 2014) was named a "Must-Read Book" by the Massachusetts Book Awards in 2015. Markell received the Barbara Bradley and Firman Houghton awards from the New England Poetry Club. Her work is included in numerous journals, including *Consequence*, *RHINO*, *Tinderbox*, *The Women's Review of Books*, and the *Compassion Anthology*. She works as a therapist with special interest in therapeutic uses of writing.

Christie Marra works as a legal aid lawyer and dance fitness instructor in Richmond, Virginia. While she loves both her social justice and fitness jobs, her true passion has always been writing and as soon as her youngest left for college she started writing fiction again. Christie's short stories have appeared in on-line journals including *Panoplyzine* and *The Write Launch* and in print in *Castabout* and *The Fredericksburg Literary and Art Review*. When she isn't writing, dancing or fighting for social justice, Christie is on a pole somewhere practicing for her next Pole Sport competition.

Martha McCollough lives in Amherst, Massachusetts. She has an MFA in painting from Pratt Institute. Her poems are forthcoming or have appeared in *Radar*, *Zone 3*, *Tammy*, *Crab Creek Review*, and *Tampa Review*, among others. Her chapbook, *Grandmother Mountain*, was published by Blue Lyra Press in October 2019.

Kevin McLellan is the author of *Hemispheres* (Fact-Simile Editions, 2019), *Ornitheology* (The Word Works, 2018), *[box]* (Letter [r] Press, 2016), *Tributary* (Barrow Street, 2015), and *Round Trip* (Seven Kitchens, 2010). He won the 2015 Third Coast Poetry Prize and Gival Press' 2016 Oscar Wilde Award, and his poems appear in numerous literary journals including *American Letters & Commentary*, *Colorado Review*, *Crazyhorse*, *Kenyon Review*, *West Branch*, *Western Humanities Review*, and *Witness*. Kevin lives in Cambridge, Massachusetts.

Deborah Mead has had stories and poems published in *Main Street Rag*, *StoryChord*, and *Iodine Poetry Review*. Her collaborative poetry chapbook, *Topless*, was published by Main Street Rag a few years ago. Her essays have appeared in the *Boston Globe*, *The Christian Science Monitor*, and Disney's *FamilyFun* magazine.

Jim Mentink's publication history has included feature pieces with NewEnglandFilm.com and the *Clovis News-Journal*. He was also a runner-up in the Eliza So 'Finish Your Book' fellowship and named an Honorable Mention in the Literary Taxidermy Short Story Contest. He was granted art residencies with Hewnoaks (2015) and Wildacres (2019) on the merit of his fiction. He's a current member of the Maine Writers and Publishers Alliance.

Myron Michael is a literary artist and producer at Move or Die, poetry collaborations. In addition to writing poetry, leading poetry workshops, making literary art, and producing literary art shows, he enjoys recording music, brand development and marketing initiatives. He invites you to visit his website at www.myronmichael.com.

Suzanne S. Rancourt is of Abenaki/Huron descent. Her *Billboard in the Clouds* (Curbstone Press) won the Native Writers' Circle of the Americas First Book Award. Her second book, *murmurs at the gate*, was published by Unsolicited Press in 2019. Her work appears in *Free State Review, Event Magazine, You Can Hear the Ocean: Anthology, Grey Borders Magazine, Synaeresis #7, Twist in Time #5, Door Is A Jar #10, Avatar Review #21, New Reader Magazine #5, Grey Borders Magazine, Big Pond Rumours, Tiny Flames Press, Quiddity, River Heron Review, The Gyroscope Review, theSame, Young Ravens Literary Review # 8, Tupelo Press Native Voices Anthology, Women of Appalachia Project, Bright Hill Press 25th Anniversary Anthology, Dawnland Voices 2.0 #4, Northern New England Review, Slipstream, Collections of Poetry and Prose, Muddy River Poetry Review, Ginosko, Journal of Military Experience, Cimarron Review*, and *Callaloo*. She is a USMC and Army Veteran.

Kat Read writes and works at GrubStreet in Boston and is a graduate of their Essay Incubator program. Her essay "The Whale" was a finalist in *Hippocampus Magazine*'s 2019 Remember in November Contest for Creative Nonfiction. Her work has appeared in *The Manifest-Station, The Sun - Readers Write, The Hunger, GRLSQUASH, Brevity Blog, Punctuate.*, and *Prometheus Dreaming*. You can find her on Twitter at @KatARead and online at www.kataread.com

Lauren Marie Scovel is a junior literary agent based in Boston. She graduated from Emerson College with degrees in Writing, Literature, Publishing, and Theatre Studies. Her editorial work can be seen at *The Millions*, and her photography can be seen on WritersResist.com.

Grace Segran has been a journalist and editor for over 25 years. She lived and worked in Asia and Europe before settling down in Boston, MA, six years ago, where she discovered creative writing at GrubStreet. Her personal essays have been published or are forthcoming in *Entropy*, *The Common*, *Westhall Press Anthology Flash Nonfiction Food*, *The Manifest-Station*, and elsewhere. She was a finalist in the *Columbia Journal* Fall 2019 Contest and won first prize in the memoir category of the 2019 Keats Literary Contest.

Alex Wells Shapiro is a poet and artist from New York, living in Chicago. He received his MFA from the School of the Art Institute of Chicago in 2017. Much of Alex's work physicalizes social and environmental relationships. He has recently published or has forthcoming work in *Tiny Seed*, *unstamatic*, *Meat for Tea*, and *Digging Through the Fat*. More of his work may be found at www.alexwellsshapiro.com.

Kerri Sonnenberg is originally from Illinois and currently lives in Cork, Ireland. Before moving to Ireland, she co-directed the Discrete Reading Series in Chicago and edited the literary journal *Conundrum*. She is the author of *The Mudra* (Litmus Press 2004). Her work has been anthologized in *The City Visible: Chicago Poetry for the New Century*, *The &NOW Awards: The Best Innovative Writing*, and most recently in *A Journey Called Home*, a collection of writing by new Corkonians.

Zachary Spence writes queer/trans*-positive fiction both short and long. An amateur (vegan) baker, he haunts the marshes of Boston with his partner and their curmudgeonly cat Jeffrey. "Baking for the Masses" is his first published piece.

Shanti Thirumalai watched the monsoon from the upper deck of BEST buses in Bombay before the city changed its name. She lives in Ann Arbor where she dabbles in classical guitar, ink painting, and child neurology. She does not have an MFA, avoids going to the gym and has no pets. She writes out of necessity.

Meg Yardley lives in the San Francisco Bay Area. Her work has recently appeared or is forthcoming in publications including *Rogue Agent*, *SWWIM*, *Bodega Magazine*, *Cagibi*, and the *Women's Review of Books*.

ABOUT PANGYRUS

Pangyrus is a Boston-based group of writers, editors, and artists with a new vision for how high-quality creative work can prosper online and in print. We aim to foster a community of individuals and organizations dedicated to art, ideas, and making culture thrive.

Combining Pangaea and gyrus, the terms for the world continent and whorls of the cerebral cortex crucial to verbal association, Pangyrus is about connection.

INDEX by AUTHOR

Author	Title	Page
V. N. Alexander	Chance that Mimics Choice	128
Diannely Antigua	Chronically	19
Mary-Kim Arnold	Legacy	171
Tanushree Baidya	Pastries in the Backcountry	113
Amy Bernstein	Hash Pipe	73
Andrea Caswell	Reciprocal Identities	174
Marisa P. Clark	Dear Life	111
Joy Cooke	Butter	183
Justin Danzy	Johnnie Redding	170
Jose Hernandez Diaz	The Most Poetic Thing	129
Franklin Einspruch	Circus Lights	138
E. Thomas Finan	The Novel I Will Never Write: A Screed By Gabe Cohen	13
Christina Marsden Gillis	The Secret Life of an Old Maine Shoe	154
David Green	Ni Pena Ni Miedo	206
Mark Halpern	The Joy of Agony	157
Michael Hardin	Northern Goshawk	181
	Eastern Owl Screech	182
Chris Hartman	Paul Laurence Dunbar Reveals How We All Wear the Mask	84
Tanya Larkin	Get Off My Lawn	20
	My Nature	23
Michael J. Leach	Black Hole Beheld	127
Ruth Lepson	The Plain	196
Flora Lindsay-Herrera	Chisinau, 2017	199
Ron MacLean	Does the Name Blackie Donovan Mean Anything To You?	61
Jennifer Markell	Up Close	151
	It's Hard to Get a Bead on God	152
Christie Marra	Longing	144
Martha McCollough	Andromeda	133
	Erinys	136
Kevin McLellan	Counting Backwards	69
	The Rise of Negation	70
	From the Inside Out	71
Deborah Mead	Moose	97

Jim Mentink	Nathaniel	189
Myron Michael	I Likened Her Hair to a River	109
Suzanne S. Rancourt	Adiabatic Theorem	82
Kat Read	Appetite	56
Lauren Marie Scovel	Off.	77
Grace Segran	Find Everything You Are Looking For?	47
Alex Wells Shapiro	Ends Meet	153
Kerri Sonnenberg	Prologue to a Stutter	186
	Forward, Thinking	187
Zachary Spence	Baking for the Masses	209
Shanti Thirumalai	Lamplight on the River	26
Meg Yardley	Appliances	195